All Is Bright

Hope and Cheer for the Christmas Season

Edited by
Marnae Kelley
Merry Gordon

pink umbrella books

©2020 Marnae Kelley and Merry Gordon
Cover & internal design ©2020 Adrienne Quintana
Cover photo © Romolo Tavani/ Adobe Stock

All rights reserved.

No part of this book may be reproduced in any for whatsoever, whether by graphic, visual, electronic, film, microfilm, tape recording, or any other means, without prior written permission of the publisher, except in the case of brief passages embodied in critical reviews and articles.

Published by Pink Umbrella Books
www.pinkumbrellapublishing.com
Kelley, Marnae, Ed.
Gordon, Merry, Ed.

All is Bright: Hope and Cheer for the Christmas Season/ Marnae Kelley, Merry Gordon

ISBN: 978-1-949598-17-9

Contents

What If?. 1

True Love Gave 8

The Inheritance of the Christmas Witch. 34

The Traditions of Isaac Stubbs. 38

The Magic of Christmastime 56

To Hope and to Dance. 59

The Christmas Dollar 66

Gingersnap Glee 76

Spreading the Spirit of Gratitude All Year Long 79

A Night at San Francisco Ballet's *Nutcracker*. *82*

A Yellowstone Christmas 87

Anonymous 114

What If?

by Michelle J. Andrew

"…in 'eav'n 'uh bells are *riiiinnnnn…iiiinnnggggg*!"

He came sliding into the kitchen at breakneck speed, screeching across the floor in a whirlwind of half-sung carol and blond curls.

"Mum! He won't let me have a turn! *Mum*!"

"Ok, okay! Hold on there just a minute!"

She put the vegetable knife down and wiped her hands on her apron.

"Now then" she said, bending down to his level to look seriously into his blue eyes, bright under the scowling frown, "what has he done this time?"

"He won't let me have a turn! He's got the controllery thing and he won't let me!"

"Yes, I will." Tig appeared at the door sullenly dragging his feet. "I never said he couldn't, I was just gonna…"

"Right, well, you've got one last chance," she said—*argh, I sound like my mother*, she thought to herself—"or the computer goes off!"

They both trawled back upstairs, muttering discontent and arguing over who was going to have the first turn.

All Is Bright

She took a deep breath and looked around the chaos of the kitchen. She had the turkey in the oven—that was done, at least—but these carrots weren't going to peel themselves. She stared down at the chopping board—hang on, hadn't she peeled one already? No, there it was, the remains of it on the kitchen floor where Brody had stolen it, eaten half of it and discarded the rest for the dog who, as if on cue, shot past her, grabbed it and flew off to the under-the-table sanctuary where she couldn't quite reach him.

"Have it, then!" she shouted after him, "and happy bloomin' Christmas!"

Right. Okay, she thought with determination, *nearly there*. The tantalising smell of roast turkey filled the kitchen, the vegetables steamed merrily on the stove and for once she hadn't overcooked the broccoli. The stuffing sat rounded and ready in six little balls and she even had the plates warming. She braced herself for the home stretch as (according to the radio for the fifth time that day) Mummy was caught

"… kissing Santa Claus…"

She gave the gravy one last stir,

"… underneath the mistletoe last night…"

tugged open the oven door,

"She didn't see me creep…"

and holding her breath,

"Down the stairs to have a peep…"

carefully… oh, so carefully…

"She thought that I was tucked up…"

drew the turkey from the oven …

"in my bedroom fast…"

as the dog flew past in a flurry of fur.

"PUT 'em UP!"—Brody, hot on his heels.

"NO, BRODY!"—Tig, racing behind.

"Not in the kitch—" They ricocheted into the oven door.

All Is Bright

"Waahhhhh!"

She wobbled backwards, catching the turkey dish just in time before the hot oil made a bid for freedom.

"…kissing Santa Claus last night!"

BANG! CRASH!

The sky exploded in a sheet of brilliance that tore through the heavens. The boys screamed and she dropped the turkey, shattering the dish on the floor as she fell backwards, arms flailing. The two boys stood stock-still, frozen in their tracks as the garden plunged into darkness. A few seconds later a low rumble stampeded across the field, thundering into a roar as the crescendo shook the house.

Staggering to her feet, she felt the tremor run deep through her bones. The little one burst into tears and with some effort, she hoisted him onto her hip. He was heavy now at four years old, like a small, dense wrecking ball. The sky lit up, illuminating a dejected turkey, an oozing, expanding puddle of oil and a halo of scattered ceramic.

CRACK!

They were plunged into darkness as the electricity gave up the ghost.

※

"When's it gonna stop?" he whimpered softly into her hair, his breath warm on her neck as he buried his head. The bell in the chapel belonging to the big house gave one solitary chime to mark the half hour. The darkened room was suspended for a moment in utter silence. *You could have heard a pin drop,* she thought, *except you never do on carpet. You just find them later when you walk on them.*

She could feel him breathing fast and trembling slightly. She shhh'd gently in his ear and rubbed his back to soothe him. And her.

"Stop being a baby," Tig muttered, but he still moved closer to her, touching her side as they stared out of his bedroom window between the curtains. *Almost as tall as me,* she thought. *Not grown up, but the man of the house now.* She put her arm around his waist.

The little one smelled of brown sugar and cinnamon, his hands still dotted with flour from his cookie baking earlier. She sat down on the edge of the window seat, bundling him onto her lap. She could feel his soft cheek sticky against her neck.

"Is…is it the end of the world?" he whispered into her hair.

She suppressed a chuckle. "No, sweetie," she reassured him, "it's just the world resting its eyes for a moment."

Tig glared through the window, transfixed by the light show, the trees stark silhouettes against the sky as the fields flashed blinding white. A bright streak shot from heaven to earth, to be lost in the distant grasses along the horizon. The fields drowned in black gloom as the booms and rumbles fought their way across the dale.

"Mum," Tig said, with a crack in his voice, "has the electricity gone off?" In horror, he glanced at his computer, which no longer held any trace of the game he'd been playing.

"Yes" she said grimly, hiding a smile and looking down at her smeared apron. *And bang goes Christmas dinner,* she thought.

They fumbled downstairs in the dark like burglars, grumbling in stage whispers.

"Who left that truck there, Brody?"

The culprit held firmly to her skirt behind her as she half tripped over the dog, who was hiding out by the door. They rummaged in the kitchen drawer and found torches, including a little whirry wind-up red one that glowed and dimmed erratically. She took a handful of candles from the dresser and (thank goodness it was still working) the lighter. They lit scented tea lights around the small living room and then lit them again after someone decided blowing them out was a

All Is Bright

fun game. The scent of cinnamon and sandalwood filled the room and made the string of festive cards and mantelpiece keepsakes flicker merrily.

"Let's light the fire, Mum!" the little one cried.

They screwed up paper and fetched in kindling, balancing it precariously in a wonky tee-pee on the grate. The lighter clicked into life and took hold of a corner of the local Echo, kissing it tenderly and igniting the heart of the little log burner. The newborn flames toddled unsteadily along its sooty walls. They tasted the edges of the paper, and then with growing confidence, nibbled tentatively at the corners of the kindling before feasting hungrily on it with crackling pops of delight. The nurtured flames raised their bright little faces—yellow, orange, red—and danced recklessly along the walls, growing and stretching to their full height, tempted to the edge of the dark chimney and flickering uncertainly beneath it before racing and roaring triumphantly upwards. They relinquished their fiery skirts. They liberated themselves from their mortal trappings. They soared up that dark passageway, gloriously escaping above the rooftops in an explosion of smoky vapour, hesitating a moment before finally surrendering to their sister stars, born again in twinkly elation to illuminate the cool night sky.

She gently pushed a log on top and stood back. The room smelled of smoke but flickered and grew warmer than was possible from just the heat of the little fire alone.

Tig pulled out the Snakes and Ladders board and the tattered dice shaker. Memories flooded her mind of childhood Christmas evenings spent with aunts and uncles, grans and grandpas, of hunting for the lost dice amid a jungle of moccasins, stockinged ankles and fluffy pink slippers in the carpeted undergrowth below the supper table.

She smiled at the memory of the well-laden drop leaf table surrounded by a mismatch of stools and chairs, little dishes of foil-wrapped toffees, Christmas crackers with soon-to-be discarded toys, remnants of coloured paper crowns that slipped over your eyes. They would clear the table to make room for the dog-eared old Snakes and Ladders board, before the hunt and victorious discovery of the dice. There were joyful squeals at the ascent of ladders and tears over the treacherous snakes, sliding down in disappointment only to roll a six and be back up and bouncing again with delight.

Later, she would be bundled up in a scratchy blanket and half asleep under a lull of hushed goodbyes, her father would lift her up into his strong arms. The cold air would whisper around them as his footsteps crunched heavily through the newly fallen snow. He would lay her curled on the backseat of the cold dark car, where she could gaze upwards through the frosted windows as the tree shadows swiped through the dark winter sky, Mum and Dad murmuring their memories in the front seats.

The dice chockled happily around inside the shaker and came to rest with a six facing cheerfully upwards.

"YES!" Tig yelled, bouncing his counter across the ever-increasing numbers. Brody watched intently, humming something about three wise men, a little donkey, and Batman.

The white rug was soft under her fingers and the glow of the smouldering logs lit up their faces. The smell of turkey and cranberry sandwiches still lingered in the air. She watched the little one. His blond head bobbed in the firelight as he dove for the dice. The dog licked his chops, looking justifiably pleased with himself for having stolen and run off with a whole turkey leg before she could stop him. Tig sprawled, head resting on one hand, concentrating on the board. He sat up cross-legged and stared into the fire as the dog came to nuzzle and root for attention under his elbow.

"Mum," he said, as she stroked the little one's soft hair, twirling her fingers in one of his curls while he snuggled warm against her, "what if the power never comes back on?"

She looked into Tig's concerned face as his eyes twinkled seriously in the flickering light.

What if? she thought…

All Is Bright
About the Author

Michelle J. Andrew spends most of her time indulging her creative inner child by covering herself in paint, glue and sawdust. She is responsible for two spirited souls of the male variety, one of 4 years and one of 11. She loves to be up to her raised eyebrows in wool, books and new hobbies, and hopes it is hereditary.

She can be found hiding in her drawing room (fondly referred to as 'Neverland'), sketching, sculpting and sewing miniature props and puppets for herself and those at the National Film School. She recently built a two-story playhouse in her living room.

Michelle lives on the bottom edge of the Peak District in rural England, surrounded by fields, sheep, two owls and one heron, with her elderly cat, Lulu, and a grey-whiskered border collie who occasionally answers to the name of Thorby.

Miss Andrew is sometimes possessed by a compulsion to write frenetic little stories involving flowery words and technicolor flights of fancy when she really should be doing less interesting things like feeding the children. Such episodes flit like butterflies across a field of poppies and she doesn't have a net in which to catch them —maybe she'll get one for Christmas.

True Love Gave

By Aaron Blaylock

'Tis the Reason

Dust shook from the sides of the old cardboard box and fell gently to the shelf. The stubborn box bowed and bent, as if resistant to the idea of being moved. He tugged a little harder and the crusty bottom slid free from its resting place.

"Pop?" a voice called from behind him. "Where you at?"

"In here."

With a grunt he heaved the box off the edge of the shelf and stepped down from the stool. A portly young man with a round face and a broad smile stepped into the doorway. Victor almost always wore that same broad smile. It was the kind of smile you could not help but return.

"Hey, Pop."

"It's 'where are you.'"

Victor tilted his head and furrowed his brow. Pop shuffled over to his workbench and softly set the fragile container down.

"'Where are you,' not 'where you at.'"

"Ah, yeah, sorry."

The top flaps of the box barely held to the sides. Gravity had done its work on the bottom edges as they curved out under the constant weight. In a whisper, almost to himself,

All Is Bright

"This is the last year." Pop squeezed the sides together and wondered how it still held. It had to have been forty years—no forty-five. *Forty-seven years*, he remembered. She used the box their toaster oven had come in, a wedding gift from Grandma Stevens. How strange that the cardboard box outlasted the toaster. It outlasted her. Tears pooled in the corners of his eyes.

"Is that the Christmas box?"

He gave a grunt and wiped at his nose with the sleeve of his flannel shirt. Carefully, he folded the flaps to either side. Inside the box, on top of a kaleidoscope of green and red, rested a nutcracker. The old wooden soldier smiled up at him with bright blue eyes.

"Lieutenant Chompers."

Pop raised an eyebrow in Victor's direction.

"That's what I call him. Momma Lou let me name him. She said it wasn't right for him to not have a name."

A knowing grin spread across his lips. That was something she would say. She named inanimate objects whether they resembled a person or not. She named his toothbrush Orwell Von Brushington. Whenever he got a new toothbrush she would just tack on another numeral. If memory served, he was using Orwell Von Brushington XCII. The grin washed from his face when met by the pain rising from his heart.

"Here, you take it."

He removed the old nutcracker from the box and offered it to Victor.

"Oh, no. I couldn't take him. She'd want him to stay with you."

"She let you name him. I think she'd want you to have him."

"Are you sure?"

Victor reached out tentatively and stroked the black boots with his finger. The paint was cracking and peeling, in need of a little tender loving care.

"I'm sure. She'd be happy to know he was taken care of."

All Is Bright

Victor accepted the gift and cradled it in the crook of his arm like an infant.

"She told me a story once about Lieutenant Chompers. Said he was handcrafted by a German carpenter somewhere in the middle of the Black Forest. He was made to be a protector. She said he guarded their homes in the Old World for a hundred years, before her great-great-grandfather brought him to America. She said he's protected the homes of her family ever since."

"And now he'll protect yours."

Victor's brown eyes glistened with tears of gratitude. Pop did not have the heart to tell him that she had found that old nutcracker at a garage sale in Sheboygan on a summer road trip back in '77. That is what she did, though—she made the most mundane things special. She made an otherwise ordinary life extraordinary.

"Thanks, Pop."

"You're welcome."

He winked and nodded at the young man. Turning back to the box, Pop pulled out the tree skirt and set it to the side.

"Do you need any help?"

"Nah, I got it."

"Oh, okay."

There was a hint of disappointment in his voice, but Pop did not want to share this with anyone. This was his time with her. It was all he had left of her. Victor was a good boy and a good helper. Pop would have gladly accepted his help raking leaves or cleaning out the gutter, but this was Christmas. Christmas was their time. It was her time. Still, a sting of pity struck him as he looked at the thick black hair on top of Victor's hung head.

"I'll tell you what, why don't you help me lug this old box inside? That would be a big help."

"Sure thing."

And just like that, Victor's broad smile lit up the dingy garage. They worked their hands beneath the crumbling

All Is Bright

cardboard box and hoisted it off the workbench. The two of them eased through the doorway and Pop could almost feel her there with them. A warm wave washed away the melancholy and for the first time in a long time he looked forward to tomorrow.

All Is Bright
One the First Day

His best guess was that he had walked up these icy steps over twenty thousand times. Mind you, they were not always icy. Sometimes they were covered in snow, sometimes they were wet with rain, and sometimes they were bone dry and hot as a skillet. He struggled to recall any time when these steps were pleasant and inviting.

"There he is. Right on time."

He had barely pulled open the door when the enthusiastic voice of Bert Mellon met him. Bert stood behind a brightly decorated counter on the other side of a plexiglass shield. Pop pulled the bandanna around his neck up over his mouth, reminded by the numerous signs posted amongst candy cane stickers. He felt like a robber in the old westerns he loved so much.

"Hey, Bert."

"Don't shoot!"

Bert threw his hands in the air. Even behind the mask he could see the smile in Bert's eyes.

"Very funny. Do you have something for me?"

"Sure do."

Bert crouched down and reached beneath the counter. He pulled out a small stack of envelopes and slipped them through the slot in the plastic barrier.

"This is it?"

"Yeah, it's even less than last year."

Pop grimaced and slipped the rubber band off the stack. Fanning them apart with his fingers, he counted eleven envelopes. Each of them had a handwritten inscription. Some were scribbled in crayon, others were carefully scrawled with pen or pencil.

"I wasn't sure we were gonna see you this year."

He looked up into Bert's red face, which reflected in the shiny foil wrapping paper on the decorative boxes to his left.

"And why's that?"

All Is Bright

Bert fidgeted with his Rudolph the Red-Nosed Reindeer pen and looked over the counter as if he had misplaced something.

"Um, well, you know. Without Lucille, I, um…I just didn't know."

The sigh escaped from his lips, along with any energy he pretended while walking up those infernal steps. Pop straightened the envelopes back into a stack and placed them in the pocket of his coat. Pausing as he turned to leave, he sighed again.

"I couldn't…."

His voice trailed off. He looked up at Bert, who was now manning the same station he had manned for over thirty-five years. The post office somehow looked smaller than he remembered. Without her, many things seemed diminished.

"I just couldn't."

He turned to leave. A gust of chilly wind awaited him on the other side of the door.

"Thanks, Bert."

"Of course. You're welcome."

His reply was barely audible between the howling wind and the closing door. Bert Mellon was a good man. He was no longer the skinny young kid Pop was saddled with as a new trainee. He had grown into his frame and his position. It was hard to tell which he had grown into more, because he had really filled out, but he was also a heck of a postman and a good friend.

Their bench awaited him, as it had year after year. At the edge of the park, next to the grand towering spruce tree. He sat on the far side of the bench, his side. The spot where she ought to be was a cold empty reminder of his loneliness. A gray sky loomed over his sadness, in stark contrast to the green and red holly and wreaths that lined Main Street. He weighed the pain he felt carrying on against the pain he would feel if he let this go, if he let her go.

"Stupid leaky nose. Ya old fool."

All Is Bright

He grumbled against himself and wiped his nose clean with the back of his cotton gloves.

"Start from the top."

That is what she would always say. *Start from the top and do what we can.* And that is exactly what he was going to do. After a brief wrestle with the first envelope, he decided that removing his gloves was both wise and necessary. She had always done the opening, even near the end when she could barely hold the envelopes. His job was to read them. He fumbled in his coat pocket for his reading glasses and finally prevailed, placing them over his hazel eyes. As if she were right there next to him, he unfolded the first letter and read aloud.

"Dear Santa, my name is Mark. I am nine years old and I don't want any kid's stuff this year. I really don't want anything for myself. What I want is for my mom to get a job. She is really sad and is always worried about food and heat. If you have a workshop near Fremont she is a really good worker. I would like to see your workshop too if I could. Really I just want her to have a job if you can do that. I have been really good and will try to be even better next year. Love, Mark Helmer."

He closed the letter and pursed his lips. Christmas shoppers passed in front of the post office, with arms full of bags and boxes. All at once he jumped to his feet and sailed across the street with a chilly winter tail wind at his back. Up the steps he went, through the door and back into the warmth of the old post office. This time he heard the ringing of the bell over the door that was drowned out by Bert's greeting earlier. "It's the Most Wonderful Time of The Year" echoed softly through the empty lobby. Bert stepped out from the back room with a snowman sugar cookie in his hand.

"Pop?"

"Hey, Bert."

"What's up?"

"Oh, uh, I...I opened the first one."

He held up the letter.

"It's from a boy. Mark. Mark Helmer. I think he and his

All Is Bright

mom live up off Birch."

"Yeah, I know 'em. Kacy, Kacy Helmer."

"That's right. Well, Mark is asking for a job for his mom. He's asking Santa for a job for his mom."

"Oh, boy. That's tough. I heard the textile factory in Oshkosh shut down. Kacy worked there. Lots of folks are out of work."

"Yeah, well, I was thinking maybe she could work here. You still take on seasonal workers for the holidays?"

"Oh, um, Pop, uh…."

"He says she's a good worker. I'll vouch for her if that helps."

"Yeah, Pop, of course that'd be great, but uh, the thing is, with everything going on it's kinda slow. We don't really have the work and even if we did there's no money. I had to move Cindy to part time last month because of budget cuts. Harold is driving for Amazon now. It's like that all over."

"Oh, I see." His eyes drifted to the long crack in the concrete floor. It was broader than he remembered. "Thanks anyway."

"I'm real sorry, Pop."

"Don't worry about it." He forced a smile. "Merry Christmas."

"Merry Christmas, Pop."

The air seemed colder and the sky darker than it had just moments ago. Lou would know what to do. She knew everybody in town, seemed like she knew everybody in the county. She would have thought of something. *What would she do? What am I gonna do?*

With no real plan, he climbed in his old pickup truck and started to drive. His memories wandered through Christmases past. Rocking horses, baby dolls, toy cars, and planes. The biggest thing he could remember was a swing set, and half the neighborhood helped with that. This seemed much much bigger than a swing set.

Not until he turned onto Birch Street did he realize where

All Is Bright

he was headed. He pulled to a stop in front of a humble two-bedroom house with a single strand of blinking lights hung over the front eave. Silence and cold poured into the cab as he turned the key. He took in a deep breath, pushed open the door and headed up the tiny walkway. A pile of leaves had gathered in the corner of the porch. A faded mat that read "Seasons Greetings" lay in front of a lopsided screen door. Pop knocked on the screen, cleared his throat and stepped back.

Anxiety gave way to panic as he heard footsteps approaching the door. Just a turn of the doorknob and a slow creak and he was looking at a woman he had not expected to be so beautiful. Lines and wrinkles marked her face, but she wore the hardship of her years well. She wore no makeup and her hair was unkempt, yet her appearance had pushed all words from his mind. She pulled her gray sweater closed and looked up into his eyes.

"Can I help you?"

"Oh, um, yeah. I mean, no. What I mean is I came to help you…to help me."

Mercifully, she did not laugh or smirk, though she did look slightly amused at his stumbling.

"Uh huh."

"My name is Charles Blake. They call me Pop."

"I'm Kacy. How can you help me, to help you, Pop?"

"Well, I heard you were looking for work, and I have a, uh, project that I need some help with."

"A project?"

"Yes, a project. I'd like to hire you to help me. I'd pay you."

"You want to pay me to help you with a project?"

"That's right."

"What's the project?"

A little boy with a full head of fluffy brown hair pushed between his mother and the door. The boy looked up at Pop and back to his mother. Pop drew in a deep breath to buy time for his mind to catch up with his mouth.

"It's, uh, a private project."

All Is Bright

"Private?"

"Yeah."

"I'm not interested in a private project, Mr. Blake."

"It's not like that, it's…."

She folded her arms and laid a scowl on him that made him want to turn and run.

"Okay, if you change your mind, you can find me over on Laird just the other side of the creek. It's the red house, needs a fresh coat of paint."

She stood as still as a statue. The sooner he got off that porch the better. He turned back to his failure waiting for him in the pickup truck. Before the idea had even fully formed, he had already turned back and started to speak.

"Listen, I really am just trying to help. Do you know Bert at the post office?"

"I don't know Bert. I went to school with Cindy, though."

"Great, go and ask Cindy about me. She knows me."

She nodded but her expression gave him no clue if she intended to follow through. He knew this year was going to be tough, but this was not at all how he imagined it going.

All Is Bright
Ten Letters Looming

A bright orange flame flickered and faded into the red-hot coals of the morning fire. Pop was sunk down into his easy chair, feeling anything but at ease. The small stack of letters sat on an end table next to a Kris Kringle letter opener and a prescription bottle, which he forgot to remember to refill. He laid a finger atop the stack and stared into the embers glowing back from the fireplace.

"I can't do this, Love. I need you."

She looked down on him from her portrait on the mantelpiece. Smiling as ever, the warmth of her goodness could not be contained by photo or frame. Stockings hung beneath her and a picture of Jesus Christ adorned the wall above her. Her image rested between two of the things she loved most. He hoped she would be happy about that.

"I miss you."

The knock at the door pulled him from his self-pity, and from his seat. With a groan, he hobbled to the front door, his knees popping and creaking louder than the floorboards. On the other side of the door, arms still folded inside the gray sweater from yesterday, stood the woman he did not think he would see again.

"Oh, um, hello."

"I spoke with Cindy."

"Oh." His voice jumped higher than he would have liked. "That's good."

"How much does this project pay?"

"Right, um, how much were you making at the factory?"

"Thirteen fifty plus benefits."

"All right, well I can't offer benefits, but I'll pay you fifteen dollars an hour."

Kacy stood silent for a moment, arms still folded, with her weight on her back foot. A truck drove by and they both glanced over at it as it passed. She turned back to him and drew in a deep breath.

All Is Bright

"What's the project?"

"Please come in."

He opened the door wider and moved to the side. Cautiously, she stepped over the threshold and made her way to the center of the room. She reminded him of a cut rose—not as vibrant and full as it had been on the bush, but still holding its beauty and majesty.

"Would you like something to drink? I make a mean cup of hot chocolate."

"No, thank you."

She looked around the living room. All at once his eyes were opened to how shabby he had let his home become. He hurried to the sofa and straightened the blue and white afghan over the back cushions.

"Please, sit."

Instead of sitting, she walked past the couch over to the mantle. She looked at the portrait of his wife and surveyed the wooden manger scene to the left of it. Pop swallowed hard and choked back tears that seemed to come from nowhere.

"Cindy said that your wife passed away."

Pop nodded.

"It'll be a year in January."

"Cancer?"

Pop nodded and swallowed hard again.

"I'm sorry."

"Me too. Thank you."

She made her way from the fireplace to the window behind the sofa, where Lou's collection of porcelain Christmas trees were displayed. Pop got nervous at the thought of one of her precious keepsakes potentially getting broken. He cleared his throat.

"Please, come and have a seat."

Kacy looked from the porcelain Christmas tree forest back to Pop.

"What's the project?"

He walked over to the end table and scooped up the stack

All Is Bright

of letters. In a single motion he slid Mark's letter from the pile with one hand and presented the letters to her with the other. She made her way around the sofa and took the opened letters from him. While she thumbed through the envelopes, Pop placed Mark's letter back on the end table beneath the Kris Kringle letter opener and sat down in his easy chair.

"We're going to answer those letters. That is, if you're willing."

Letter in hand, she sat on the edge of the sofa.

"You know, I met your wife a half dozen times. She was Mrs. Claus at the school, for breakfast with Santa."

Pop gave a nod. He remembered her, set in the bustle of the school cafeteria, dressed like an elf covered from head to toe in green and red. She was so happy to be surrounded by excited children, with Christmas music blaring over the intercom.

"I remember her being so kind to my son. I wish I had known her better."

Pop looked to the floor in the corner of the room and fought against the tears pooling in his eyes. He wished for the days when tears did not come so easily. His sleeve once again served as a snot squeegee and he tried to move the conversation forward.

"I dressed as Santa once when Hank couldn't do it. She had to stuff my coat with pillows so this old bag of bones could pass for the big fella. It didn't take long for a tubby third grader to climb up on my lap and squish that pillow right out the bottom of my jacket. Lou had to move fast to distract the kids while I shoved my padding back in place."

Kacy smiled and was all the prettier for it. He wondered if she got to smile very often these days. With the state of things there were not a lot of smiles to go around. Pop decided right then to look for more reasons to smile.

"Okay, I'm in. But I need to be home by dinner. My folks are watching Marky, but evenings are our time."

"Deal."

"Where do we start?"

All Is Bright

"We start from the top and do what we can."

He gestured to the stack in her hands. She opened the first envelope and pulled out the letter. Clearing her throat, she read out loud.

"Santa, my name is Molly. I just turned six. I am good. How are you? I would like a tea set and a friend. Thank you. Molly."

She let the letter rest in her lap, cradling it in her hands.

"Oh my gosh, what do we do?"

"Well, I have Lou's tea set that I'm sure she'd be happy to give. But first we need to find out where Molly lives."

"What about the friend?"

"We do what we can."

She nodded thoughtfully.

"Okay, I'll ask around and see what I can find out."

Without hesitation, she moved to the next letter on the pile. Pop got up from his chair and placed a block of wood atop the still glowing embers. He shoved some kindling between the cold log and the warm coals. *This fire is not out yet.*

All Is Bright
Little Saint Rick

"All right, I found a plush Baby Yoda doll, the kind with the soft head, on eBay for twenty-five bucks with free shipping. I don't think we're gonna beat that deal anywhere. I've ordered it and it should be here by Tuesday. I know that's cutting it close, but I think we'll be okay."

Pop listened as she rattled off words he did not fully understand, but he was satisfied they all sounded like good news.

"I spoke to Nathan's mom and she is emphatic that she does not want him to have a BB gun, so I don't know what you're going to do there."

"I'm working on it right now."

He held up the long wooden rod he was sanding down. One of his few talents was woodworking. Lou always said it was his God-given gift, like the carpenter of Nazareth. He had worked half the night to carve that old piece of balsa wood into a genuine-looking toy rifle. Nathan said he wanted a BB gun to play soldier. Pop figured he could still play soldier with a wooden gun and his mother would not have to worry about him shooting the neighbor's dog.

"Great. I still haven't been able to locate our six-year-old Molly, but I'm working on it. I'm going to meet Rickey's mom at the playground. He and Marky are friends and I thought it would be a good chance to talk with her and an excuse to spend a little time with Marky."

"Sure, fine. That's great."

"Would you like to come along?"

Pop quit sanding and looked across the garage. Kacy stood back in the doorway, wearing the same gray sweater as always and a pair of thick boots that came up to her ankles. He considered her offer and how to politely say no. Not only was he anxious to finish the rifle but he really wanted to lie down for a while and rest. Still, it had been a while since he had been invited anywhere, and by a beautiful woman, nonetheless.

All Is Bright

"You could meet my son. You didn't really get to say hi when you came by the house. He's a real good kid."

Pop placed the wooden rifle on his workbench and rubbed his dusty hands on his pants.

"When are you going?"

"I'm going to pick up Marky right now."

Pop nodded and shook the sawdust from the front of his flannel jacket. He grabbed his hat and followed Kacy to her little blue hatchback car parked just outside the garage. Looking in the back window he could see shoes, socks, papers, and an empty McDonald's carton. He paused when confronted with a similar assortment of wrappers, cartons, and cables awaiting him in the front seat.

"How about I drive?"

Kacy was rummaging through her purse.

"Sure."

Relieved, Pop led the way to his pickup truck and opened the passenger side door for Kacy.

"Well, thank you. Such a gentleman."

She touched him softly on the arm as she climbed in the truck. He resisted the urge to skip around to the driver's side. Not only because of how it would look but because he was likely to pop a hip out of place or something. In any case, he did not need that embarrassment.

"My parents' place is on the other side of town. On Theodore, just off of Main."

"Got it."

Without even asking, Kacy reached over and turned on the radio. She tuned into a station playing Christmas music and the smooth tones of Bing Crosby singing "Happy Holidays" came flowing into the cab. The only other person who had ever helped herself to his radio was his wife. It would have bothered him, it should have bothered him, but it did not.

"Lou loved Bing Crosby, but not half as much as she loved Dean Martin."

"Two of the greats."

All Is Bright

"I used to joke with her that she'd leave me for Dean if she got the chance. She'd say it'd be a shame to leave me after all the work she did house breaking me."

He chuckled and she laughed. It felt good to laugh again. Out of the corner of his eye, he caught a glimpse of her smile. He wondered how a lady like this could be single, but he was too nervous to ask.

"Christmas Eve, after we'd delivered all the presents, I'd make up a fire and some hot chocolate. Lou would put on her favorite record and we'd dance to Dean singing "Silver Bells." Don't know that Christmas gets any better than that. I didn't even mind Dean butting in on our dance."

"That sounds lovely."

Her son came bounding down the driveway almost before the truck came to a stop. She squatted down and gave him a big hug, then ushered him to the opened door.

"Pop, this is Marky."

"Mom, don't call me Marky."

"I forgot, Mr. Grown-up. Pop, this is Mark."

"How do you do, Mark?"

"Just fine. Nice to meet you."

"The park is just up around the corner. Pam said she'd be there about now."

Mark squeezed in the middle between them, and Pop backed out of the driveway.

"So, Mark, what's your favorite subject in school?"

"P.E."

Kacy rolled her eyes and Pop chuckled.

"That was my favorite too. I was the only one in my class that got to the top on the rope climb. Lou joked that was my highest academic achievement."

"Cool."

"That's Pam right there, and there's Rickey."

Mark squeezed by his mother as soon as the truck stopped and ran to his friend. Kacy followed after him, and Pop hung back by the truck. He watched the children running and playing

All Is Bright

around the frozen monkey bars and swings. Several children dug in the cold sand while their parents visited between the leftover patches of slush from the last snow.

Two solitary figures caught his eye at the far end of the playground. A little girl in a fluffy pink coat sat on the curb with her feet in the sand. She pushed the sand around listlessly with her boots while she watched the other children playing. A few feet away, a woman sat alone on a bench staring blankly at the little girl. He felt drawn to them and found himself wandering in their direction.

"Pam is a no on the drums."

He had not seen Kacy approaching and her voice startled him.

"What?"

"Drums, for Rickey. His mom says no."

"Oh, um, okay."

"We'll figure something out. I heard there are drum pads with headphones. That might work."

Pop was still studying the little girl and the woman on the bench.

"Who's that?"

"I don't know, but they look like they could use some company."

"Why don't you go over there?"

"That wouldn't look right, some old guy just walking up to them in the park."

"Yeah, that'd be awkward, like some old guy knocking on your door and offering to pay you for a secret project."

He found her wearing the smirk he deserved on her charming face.

"Go talk to her, you old coot."

"I think you should go."

She shook her head and punched him softly on the shoulder.

"Fine."

Pop followed behind her at a distance as she sat down on the bench next to the woman. He watched anxiously as the two

All Is Bright

of them began to talk. The woman nodded and pointed to the little girl in the pink jacket. Kacy turned around and waved Pop over. Tentatively, he made his way to the women on the bench.

"Hey Pop. This is Helen and her daughter, Molly."

She placed emphasis on Molly and looked up at him with widened eyes. He met her gaze with wide eyes of his own. The girl looked to be six years old or so. Pop struggled to wrap his mind around this happy coincidence.

"They just moved here from Janesville."

"Pleased to meet you."

"Pleasure, ma'am."

Mark and Rickey made their way around the monkey bars and over to the little girl in the pink jacket. They plopped down in front of her and began to draw in the sand. Rickey looked up from his drawing at Molly.

"I like your jacket."

"Thank you."

Molly hung her hooded head.

"Is it warm?"

"Yes."

"Do you like Pokémon?"

"No."

"Do you like Minecraft?"

"No."

"Do you want to play tag?"

"Okay."

The boys stood up and reached out to Molly. She grabbed their hands and they pulled her to her feet. The three of them walked back toward the monkey bars. Mark gave Rickey a push.

"You're it."

They began to laugh and run in all directions. Several other kids joined in. In moments, smiles and laughter filled the park. Helen pulled a tissue from her purse and started to cry. Kacy put an arm around her and gave her a squeeze. Pop watched the children play and smiled.

"We're getting that boy his drums."

All Is Bright
God Rest Ye Merry, Gentleman

Ten meticulously wrapped, brightly colored, packages were piled neatly in the corner of the living room. The meticulous wrapping was entirely the work of Kacy. Lou had always been the wrapper and Pop struggled to get the bends and folds to look as neat and clean as she did.

"That's it. We did it."

"All that's left is to take them around when it gets dark."

"We should celebrate. How about that hot chocolate I've heard so much about?"

"You got it."

Pop sauntered into the kitchen beaming with pride and joy. He placed a pot on the stove and fired up the burner. Grateful he remembered to buy milk yesterday, he pulled open the fridge.

"Mind if I put on some music?"

"Sure thing. There's a box of records beneath the player."

Several minutes later he heard Perry Como and the Fontane Sisters singing "It's Beginning to Look a Lot Like Christmas." It was the first song on Lou's favorite album. Bubbles formed across the surface of the milk. Pop carefully poured the boiling milk into mugs with chocolate waiting at the bottom. He grabbed a spoon, stirred them up and headed back into the living room.

Kacy stood in the center of the room with an unfolded letter in her hand. His gaze fell on the empty end table next to his easy chair. She looked up from the letter with tear-soaked eyes. He placed the piping hot mugs on the dining room table and shuffled side to side as he waited for words, his or hers, to come.

"This is my Marky. He asked for this?"

Pop nodded. Unsure whether to apologize or not, he just stood still.

"And you did this for him?"

Tears flowed freely now. He wanted to comfort her but

was still uncertain where he stood. Was she grateful, or upset at him for not being forthcoming? For all his years he was never good at discerning between tears of sadness and tears of joy.

"Kacy, I...."

Words failed him. He stepped into the living room, not knowing what to do or say. She set the letter back on the end table. He moved as far as the rug and stopped. Without a word, she bounded toward him and embraced him with a big bear hug. After he recovered from the fright of her sudden movement, Pop placed his arms around her and held her close while she sobbed.

"You let me think I was helping you."

"You helped me more than you know."

She looked up at him and he brushed a lone strand of hair from her flushed face. Just then Dean began to sing about city sidewalks, busy sidewalks. Kacy rested her head on his shoulder and he held her a moment longer. They began to sway gently to the melody of "Silver Bells." Pop felt a closeness that he had only shared with one other. He jumped back and pushed her away.

"No, this is...no."

"Pop, I'm sorry, I didn't mean...."

"You should go."

"Pop, please...."

"Just go, please."

This time he had little doubt the origins of those tears. He did not want to hurt her, but his shame could not bear her presence. She gathered up her purse and sweater and pulled open the front door. Without looking back at him, she paused.

"Pop, thank you for everything. I am truly sorry. I never meant...I, I'm sorry."

The crack in her voice was like a dart to his heart. And with that she was gone. He stood in an empty room. Just him and Dean, still crooning on about those silver bells. He walked over to the record player and pulled the needle from the vinyl. The portrait of his beloved wife smiled down on him and his guilt

All Is Bright

bubbled over into tears.

"Forgive me, Love."

He turned away from the fireplace and noticed the letter from the end table had blown to the floor. On impulse alone he stooped down and picked it up. He held Mark's letter in his hands and looked at the carefully crafted message. Instantly he was encircled in love. He felt his wife's love for him, and for children, and for Christ, and for Christmas. He felt his love for Mark, and for Kacy, and for Molly, and for Rickey, and for Nathan, and for all the children they had given to over the years. For the first time, he felt all that those people had given to them without even knowing it. Like a ribbon, love flowed through the letter and bound him to so many. Looking up to the mantelpiece into the face of his bride, he felt her there with him.

"Look at all you gave."

The most exquisite feeling of gratitude and joy came over him.

"Thank you, Love."

He basked in that love another moment before the image of Kacy's tear-stained face returned to his mind. Dusk had settled on the world outside his window. Pop grabbed a pencil from the end table and hurried to the dining room. He turned Mark's letter over and began to write.

When he finished, he pulled out his wallet and folded a stack of cash in the letter and returned it to the envelope. Quickly, he loaded up the gifts for the children in the back of his truck and climbed in the cab just as snowflakes began to fall from the sky. He muttered a curse and hurried back into the garage. He found the tarp and some rope and rushed back to protect the precious packages. His heart pounded hard in his chest and he struggled to draw in full breaths. He said a prayer that God would let him deliver these presents and he started up the old pickup.

His circuitous route took him past her house several times. Each time he looked down at the letter in the passenger's seat.

All Is Bright

Each time he considered stopping. Each time he drove on to the next house on the list.

The snow was falling heavy and his wiper blades were hardly up to the task. He had to roll down the window to clean the windshield with his hand. The chill stung his ear and cut right through his flannel jacket. He pressed on, in spite of the cold and ignoring the pains in his chest, until the bed of the truck was empty and all that was left was a tattered envelope on the seat next to him.

He trudged up to the porch of the darkened house. If he was being honest, he was relieved that it appeared no one was home. He tucked the envelope snuggly under the Seasons Greetings mat and shuffled through the snow back to his truck. After several purposeful breaths, he felt a burden lift from his shoulders.

"We did it, Lou."

He took one last look at the tiny home, with the single strand of blinking lights over the eave, before he put the truck in gear and headed for home. The road was no longer visible no matter how well he wiped the windshield with his gloved hand. His tires lost traction as they found the edges of a ditch next to the road. Pop was powerless to stop both wheels on the right side from slipping all the way into the ditch. He pressed on the accelerator to no avail. The night was growing colder by the minute. Less than a mile from the house he decided his best option was just to walk home, get warm, and come back in the light of day.

"Stupid white Christmas."

He muttered to himself, standing knee deep in snow. With his jacket buttoned up all the way and his hat pulled down over his ears, he waded through the muck. His joints ached until he felt they might burst. It felt as if the snow had sucked all the oxygen out of the air. The chill stung his lungs and pained his chest.

"Almost there."

The porchlight from his house shone like a beacon

All Is Bright

through the snowy night. He drew closer and caught sight of a blue hatchback in his driveway. With his eyes set on the unexpected sight, he stumbled to one knee and caught a face full of powdery snow. Two shadowed figures approached from the house.

"Pop!"

Kacy pressed through the knee-deep snow and helped him to his feet. Mark was just behind her and caught Pop by the elbow to steady him. A pain caught him in the chest and he winced in agony.

"Why didn't you come get me?"

"I thought you were done with me."

"Let's get you inside and get you warm, you old coot."

They helped Pop through the door and set him down gently in his easy chair.

"Mark, see if you can get that fire going. I'm going to make you a warm drink."

He caught Kacy by the arm. She spun around and looked down at him with her soft brown eyes. Pop took one last long look.

"You did more for me than I did for you."

"Just rest, Pop. I'll be right back."

"It's okay, I'm okay. I just wanted to thank you and say I'm sorry."

"You've got nothing to be sorry for. I'm the one who is sorry."

"No. No, you shouldn't be. I just loved her so much. I love her so much."

"I know. I know you do."

The warmth of the fire reached him and the light bathed Kacy in its glory.

"That's all I feel now. Love. Love and gratitude."

"That's great, Pop, but you need to feel warmth. Mark, get him that blanket."

Mark hurried over with the afghan from the sofa. He gently placed it over his shoulders and Pop let go of Kacy's arm.

All Is Bright

"I feel warmth. I feel her warmth."

"Keep that fire going, I'll be right back."

Kacy ran to the kitchen and Mark placed another log on the fire. Pop sank down into his easy chair and closed his eyes. The room started to turn slowly, and he could hear the echoing tones of Dean serenading them. From the depths of his heart he heard the voice of his one true love. *That's enough. You started from the top and you did what you could.* A smile broke across his face.

"Soon it will be Christmas day."

He sang softly and fell into a sweet deep sleep.

All Is Bright
About the Author

Aaron Blaylock is the author of *The Land of Look Behind* and *The Unsaid*. Born and raised in Arizona, Aaron is proud to call the desert home. He came of age in the suburbs of Sacramento, California, and as a missionary for The Church of Jesus Christ of Latter-day Saints in Jamaica, where he fell in love with the people and their culture, but he has always been drawn back to the Valley of the Sun.

He married his childhood crush, the girl of his dreams, in 2001. Together they are raising four beautiful and rambunctious children. He worked as a freelance sports reporter for *The Arizona Republic* for nearly ten years, combining his love of writing and sports. When not working, writing or serving at church, Aaron volunteers as a soccer and baseball coach for his children and enjoys chasing a small white ball around a golf course.

His storytelling draws heavily from his love of history, adventure, his faith and his own life experiences.

The Inheritance of the Christmas Witch

By Lauren Cutrone

When I personify Christmas, she's a woman far bolder than myself. She's tall and plump and doesn't apologize for taking up too much space. Her glasses are rimmed with a shade of burgundy, or perhaps a pattern of tortoiseshell, and she wears kitten heels—not because she needs the height but simply because she likes how they make her feel. She's a powerhouse, Miss Christmas. Whereas if I were a holiday, I'd be something far quieter. Arbor Day or Palm Sunday. Something worthy of a celebration but too meek to make much of a fuss about it.

I admire Christmas for its colorful nature and for its megaphone audacity. But, meek as I was and continue to be, I never found myself understanding Christmas. I didn't have much of a say in the matter—as a granddaughter of proud Roman immigrants, I was confirmed into the Catholic faith where Christmas is sort of a big deal. It stumbles in every year, always sooner than I'm ready for, and hangs up its coat, expecting tea before my kettle is even on the burner.

My relationship with Christmas is complex and strained. We don't see eye to eye on most issues and we certainly don't tackle life with the same attitude. But I have a feeling Christmas

All Is Bright

isn't going anywhere. I can either hide from the holiday each year (easier said than done) or learn to appreciate it. I chose the latter. And to find something I did understand, my struggle came full circle and met my Italian heritage again.

As a little girl, I developed a thirst for knowledge that, to this day, is unquenchable. What I felt was something akin to envy. If Katelyn in Kindergarten was taking ballet lessons, I too had to take ballet lessons. If Jessica in first grade was taking gymnastics lessons, I too had to take gymnastics lessons. It was only natural that when I entered the second grade and learned that Grace was taking Italian lessons, I too had to take Italian lessons. This one, unlike the others, didn't take much convincing. My mother was thrilled that her daughter took an interest in the language she was blanketed in as a child.

(To ruin the ending of that story, I'm not fluent. I'm more like a four-day drive and a boat trip away from fluency. My tutor taught me to say words like grape and tiger. Window and television. But ask me to string together a sentence and I'm hopeless. Make a trip to Italy and you'd better ask someone else to be your guide.)

For whatever reason, I remember one lesson better than all the others—and it had nothing to do with the Italian language. No, this had to do with the celebration of Christmas in Italy and the veneration of a mythical being known as La Befana. A bigger deal than Babbo Natale, Italy's version of Santa Claus, La Befana is instead a Christmas witch who does the distribution of gifts around the holidays. My tutor taught me that she would leave oranges in your shoes if you were good but I hear this has been updated to candy and toys. She appreciates if you leave her some wine and food to sustain her for her long journey by broomstick. But before she goes, she'll use her broomstick to sweep up your floor. Like Santa Claus, she goes unseen. Her deeds are hidden from the recipients of her gifts. She gathers the gifts, she offers you food, she cleans up the mess, and she goes on her way.

As I grew, I saw La Befana in every woman I knew. I

saw her in the women who went from store to store to store to find that perfect Furby doll. I saw her in the women who spent hours over a hot stove to make the antipasto, the savory main course, the decadent desserts. I saw her in the women on their hands and knees, scrubbing the bathroom floor until it smelled like bleach and cleanliness. I saw La Befana in my mother, my aunts, my grandmother, my great aunts. I feel her moving in and making herself at home within my bones. And I feel myself encouraging her to take a seat and asking her to stay a while.

There's something about women around the holidays. They become Amazons. They take on a workload made for a family of twenty and perhaps a few workhorses and they do it all without complaint. They do it not for money or glory or reciprocity of gifts. They do it all to see the glowing smiles and to hear the jovial laughter of those they hold most dear.

It's this, I've realized, I love more than anything else about the holidays. More than the gingerbread and the candles and the hymns and the ugly sweaters, I love the unseen women who work tirelessly to make one single day, a day we repeat each and every year, so memorable. I still can't say I understand the closeness to the holiday, but I understand beyond anything else the love and appreciation for these superhero women who give everything they have to create something magical.

This very well might be my inheritance. One day, I will be one of these women. I will be left to carry on a celebration filled with tenderly sewn stockings and sizzling breakfast sausages and a tree adorned with countless mismatched ornaments. And though the thought makes me tremble, though I have a few years before I will be ready, I can't help but smile and welcome the gracious, loving, and selfless Christmas witch who brews inside of me.

All Is Bright
About the Author

Lauren Cutrone currently works for Princeton University. She has previously been published as a poet and essayist in books such as Alcott's Imaginary Heroes: The Little Women Legacy, Women Speak: Portraits, Poetry, and Prose of the Feminine Experience, and Notable American Women Writers. She lives in New Jersey near the loveliest farms and apple orchards and spends her time baking, meditating, reading, and listening to opera.

The Traditions of Isaac Stubbs: Being a Ghost Story for Christmastime

By N.A. Kimber

In loving memory of Michael Donoghue, who loved to tell stories and was fond of Christmas

Our story begins with a Christmas Eve not unlike this one, where family and friends sat gathered around the fire and shared a ghost story. It took place in a small town of little consequence, except to those who lived there, by the name of Burwick. It was a lively little town for its population, but it was a place filled with love and laughter, particularly on Christmas Eve.

The adults all sat happily drinking mulled wine and cider and the children all huddled together beneath woolen blankets as old Mistress Mason crooned out the story of Gabriel Grubb and the goblins who stole him away. A thin but highly decorated tree rested in the corner of the ballroom, whose floors were worn from the years of dancing. Just beneath the tree branches sat a deep green chest, always locked, with a bright red bow and holly berries.

Trimmings of spruce and pine branches hung from the walls. Above the entrance dangled the most beautiful and vibrant sprig of mistletoe, under which more than a few young lovers had caught themselves. Small scraps of cheese

All Is Bright

twists, candied orange peels, mincemeat tarts, ginger molasses biscuits and rose Turkish delight lay across silver plated trays upon the oak table against the far wall, having been enjoyed and consumed heartily. To the good people of Burwick, it was a Christmas Eve that would have made the hearts of Dickens and Irving warm at the sight.

And at the center of it all was Isaac Stubbs.

Isaac Stubbs, who on this Christmas Eve had reached the comfortable age of sixty, was quite possibly the kindest man the small town had ever known. He had moved to Burwick nearly ten years prior in the early spring. No one knew if he had ever had a wife or children, and since he never spoke of it, no one ever asked. All they had ever known was that he had had some kind of falling out with his eldest brother and soon found himself in Burwick. Upon arriving with a good deal of wealth he had done two things almost immediately: he had opened up the finest cabinetry shop the town had ever seen, and he had purchased and moved into the old Carter Manor, which had been abandoned for ten years since the family had moved into a larger city north of the river.

The town of Burwick had grown to love him quickly, as he made beautiful furniture and wares for the adults and always threw in a small wooden toy for the children. He attended church each Sunday and his soaring voice could be heard above all others in the congregation. He took on many young men as apprentices, who soon grew as fine in skill as him. His smile always reached his eyes and his laugh could brighten any solemn day. He was a man who loved the town and its people well, and he showed it in nearly all aspects of his life.

That was why, as the winter came around the first year many years ago, the townspeople were greeted with singular surprise and delight to an invitation to the old Carter Manor for a Christmas Eve party. The news of such an event had caused quite the uproar in town. Many of the townsfolk approached Isaac and asked if he was certain he was prepared to host the entire community. He had only smiled and repeated

All Is Bright

the sentiment written on each and every invitation: "All who come with love in their hearts are welcome."

So began the tradition of the town of Burwick gathering in Isaac Stubbs' home and celebrating Christmas Eve.

It was a wonderful tradition that they enjoyed for many years, and there were some who as children had enjoyed Isaac Stubbs' hospitality who had grown old enough to now bring their own children to experience the joy. The Christmas Eve party became an event the whole town looked forward to every year, and they would each make decorations, bake delicious treats and meet at the church before making the short walk to Carter Manor, singing Christmas carols along the way and knowing they were close when they heard Isaac join in. He would shake each of their hands and welcome them warmly. For the town of Burwick, Isaac Stubbs and Christmas were one and the same.

This was why, when in the summer just over six years from the beginning of our story, before his sixty-seventh birthday, the entire town was struck in deep mourning when he passed away. He had gone gently into the night, no one in the town having known or suspected any chance of death. Mr. Clark, the owner of the mill, had visited him just the day before to pick up a set of wooden soldiers for his son Charles' birthday, and, his hand to God, had claimed the man had seemed as fit and healthy as a young man in his prime. Nonetheless, Isaac Stubbs had passed. It was not often that a man had an entire town lay him to rest, but Isaac Stubbs was one of those fortunate and well-loved few.

Some weeks had passed after his death before a letter arrived in the mail for the Reverend Thomas, who had been reading quietly in his office when Miss Hollin, who worked at the post office, had come running into the church. She was panting and out of breath, but in her hand she held a worn envelope with the reverend's name in fine black ink. The back showed that it had been sent by Isaac Stubbs.

When the congregation gathered the following Sunday, the

All Is Bright

whole room was alive with chatter and gossip. Everyone was aware of the letter's existence, for privacy was never a factor in a town so closely knit, particularly when Ms. Hollin was around. When the reverend finally stepped onto his podium, the whole room fell silent, eyes now focused upon the set of yellow pages within his hands.

The letter was short and simple and so the reverend read it aloud to the entire congregation.

To my dear friends,

My time is coming to an end and I only wish to express that I have enjoyed our moments together. I have left all that I have to my niece, Bathsheba, a bright young girl with much ahead of her. Though I have not seen her in many years, we have spoken frequently in the last few months. She has many affairs to settle before she makes the journey and so I have left the key to my home with the good Reverend Thomas, who will give it to Bathsheba upon her arrival. Until that time, as always, all who come with love in their hearts are welcome. Bathsheba has been made aware of my traditions and I have implored her to carry them on, should she wish to fulfill my final wishes. I beg of you to welcome her as you welcomed me all those years ago. May you enjoy this Christmas Eve and those to come on my behalf, for I shall always be with you.

Your Friend,
Isaac Stubbs

And so, as Isaac had wished it, the entire town worked to make sure Carter Manor was ready for Christmas Eve. They cleaned the now empty home from top to bottom and decorated it until it came alive with the spirit of Christmas. They baked their delicious treats and touched up their Sunday bests. When Christmas Eve arrived, the Reverend Thomas led the walk from the church to Carter Manor, the entire town singing as they went. While Isaac was gone, some could swear they still heard the answering call of Isaac's singing voice as they drew closer to the manor. The reverend had the key in hand and when they reached the home, he unlocked it slowly. Soon the warmth of memory and love washed over them. Despite the loss of the great host, it ended up being a beautiful Christmas Eve and all the town knew that Isaac Stubbs was there, celebrating with them.

This continued for a few more years, much to the surprise of the town, who had been expecting Bathsheba Stubbs in the early spring. Yet it was not until nearly the autumn before the fourth Christmas without Isaac that she came knocking upon the reverend's door, asking in a clipped tone for the key to her uncle's manor. While the reverend had only known Isaac in his later half of life, he was startled by the similarities of their features. They had the same crooked nose that rounded at the tip and the same rich shade of chestnut hair, although Isaac's had gone fully white come the end of his days. Her fingers were also long and thin and her lips small and slightly pouting, but he could tell that they, along with the familiar chocolate eyes, would be beautiful and welcoming once she smiled with true joy.

She moved into the home quickly, having only brought a single trunk with her. She had come to the reverend one Sunday after mass and asked him for the key to the green chest, long since removed of its holly berries and bow. The reverend told her he had no such key, and it hurt him to see her walk away disappointed.

To the town's unparalleled joy, she reopened her uncle's cabinetry shop, hiring some of the local men who had once been Isaac's apprentices to do some of the more difficult work. She dropped in once a week and delivered wooden toys that she had carved herself. They were not as detailed as Isaac's had been, but they were made with the same care and love. She was a dressmaker by trade, and so many of the women and young girls were given the opportunity to know her. She held

All Is Bright

a quiet disposition quite different from her uncle. She worked seriously and diligently, hardly taking the time to initiate or carry a conversation. Still, she was a reminder of Isaac and his legacy. Her voice, too, rang out stronger than any others as the congregation sang on Sundays.

This familiarity and the love the town held for Isaac was what caused Reverend Thomas to approach the young mistress of Carter Manor and discuss her uncle's annual tradition.

"It has been a staple of our town for nearly twenty years, thanks to your beloved uncle, God bless his soul," he began, smiling softly at the young woman. "Everyone bakes and helps to decorate, and it truly brings us all together. The letter your uncle sent me following his death assured me that he would implore you to continue the tradition."

"It was mentioned in the letter he sent to me along with the deed to the house; however, Reverend Thomas, I do not believe that I shall follow in my uncle's footsteps." She said it quite plainly, without any bite to her voice, but she watched as the reverend's face fell.

"I cannot pretend I am not disappointed," the reverend began. "May I ask why?"

"My uncle loved Christmas, Reverend Thomas. I have known that since I was a child. Once he moved to Burwick, any kind of celebration came to an end. Once Uncle Isaac took his share of the family fortune and left, my father saw no point in carrying it on. My grandfather had never made a show of Christmas. Uncle Isaac had just read too much Dickens and Irving and my father allowed him to entertain us. I have not celebrated a Christmas since I was seven years of age, and I do not intend to begin again, all because Uncle Isaac had a foolish argument with my father. My uncle left us and took Christmas with him, and in that regard, I will not celebrate that for which he forsook me." With a quick bow of her head she ended the conversation with a "Good day, Reverend Thomas," before she turned on her heel and walked out of the church.

A cloud of melancholy fell over the town, as the beloved

All Is Bright

Christmas tradition was brought to an abrupt end. Reverend Thomas had attempted to suggest that they celebrate together in the church, but old Mistress Mason, now eighty-three, protested greatly. "We are supposed to be in Carter Manor. That is where Isaac would have wanted us. I do not want to be celebrating where he cannot find us." The town all solemnly agreed. So it came to pass that for the first time in twenty years, not one member of the town of Burwick prepared to celebrate Christmas Eve.

When the day finally arrived the town was eerily still. Christmas Eve day had not been a silent affair in so long that one could not help but be aware of all that was missing. The weather itself seemed to take on the mood as the wind refused to blow, and not a drop of snow fell from the sky. The white blanket that had fallen the day before remained untouched and stagnant. All the townspeople remained inside of their homes, doing their best to enjoy their Christmas Eve as they mourned the loss of a well-loved tradition and a well-loved man.

Bathsheba Stubbs sat comfortably by her fire that Christmas Eve, unaware, in part, of the amount of turmoil she had caused in Burwick. Hardly being able to remember her Christmas Eves with her Uncle Isaac aside from the bitterness she felt at his departure, she could not possibly grasp what a gift she had taken away from the community. So for a time, she sat contentedly, as though it were any other evening, and began to nod off by the roaring fire.

As we know, Christmas is a time for ghosts and goblins alike. They do not come when people make merry, but find those hearts without an ounce of Christmas spirit in the beat and show them the truth hidden by their ignorance. Is this not what we all have been waiting for as we gather around the fire, listening for the howling of the wind, a creak in the floorboards, a moan from the attic, a scratching at the window?

Bathsheba Stubbs had no such greeting, nothing so startling as to make her heartbeat wild and her mind scattered. No, instead Bathsheba was awoken to a sound that was familiar

All Is Bright

to Carter Manor on Christmas Eve, and this was the sound of carols.

The voices were so quiet at first that they did not stir her completely. Rather, they filtered their way into her dream, which had once been a blank space of white and now filled with memory of sweet shortbread and her father playing the piano as Uncle Isaac sang. Her younger sister sat under the tree, pulling pieces of popcorn onto a string. Her mother hung baked gingerbread men onto its branches, humming along to the music. All that had faded when Uncle Isaac had moved away, and though she was asleep and would soon forget it, her heart ached just a touch to have the moment back. Uncle Isaac's voice was soon joined by others, growing louder and echoing in the corners of her mind, until they shook the confines of the dream and made the images blur.

Bathsheba awoke violently, letting out a gasp as she surged out of her chair, nearly stumbling towards the hearth. The voices sang loudly and beautifully, the lyrics of "O Come, All Ye Faithful" flowing through the locked windows and doors. Swallowing deeply, Bathsheba approached the windows of the drawing room, confused and still partially in the realm of dreams. She wiped away at the fog that had gathered upon the glass, trying to peer out to see the figures to which the voices belonged.

The field beyond was dark and as far as her eyes could see, there was not a soul in sight.

The singing grew louder and Bathsheba tore to the front door, undid the latch and pulled it open wide, gazing out into the cold winter night in nothing more than her white nightgown and her Uncle Isaac's red flannel blanket wrapped around her shoulders.

The song echoed across the open plain, not a light or a shadow out of place. The wind did not blow and no snow fell. There was only the darkness of the night and the chorus echoing its song.

"Hello?" Bathsheba called, but the only answer was the

All Is Bright

song, growing louder with each passing second. She slammed the door shut, pressing her back to it and trying to shake the noise from her head. She wrapped the blanket tighter around her frame to fight the chill that had overtaken the house.

She moved back to the fire, settling into the plush armchair once more, and attempted to bring the feeling back to her bare feet, wiggling her toes gently. The fire roared, larger than when she had left it, but it produced little heat. The chill from the outside permeated the room and sank into her bones. The singing only grew louder, until it seemed as though the voices were right outside her front door.

The door banged open, causing Bathsheba to jump in her seat with a loud scream. The singing came to an abrupt and chilling halt.

An empty house is known to creak and perhaps at times moan, but the stairs seldom feel the weight of footsteps on their own, and a door can scarcely hold itself open without someone standing there to keep it in place. And yet, invisible feet ascended the stairs as the open door welcomed them in.

Bathsheba felt a heaviness in her legs as her throat grew tight. She rose from her chair once more and approached the door. The golden knocker glared angrily at her in the dim light and she felt the cold air as it seeped in, wrapping around the skin of her calves and up her legs, like the ivy that had creeped up the side of the manor in the warmer months. As she approached the door, she saw the latch lift itself up and down, as though someone were playing with it. One long, thin hand outstretched, Bathsheba reached for the door. Once she had grabbed its edges, she tried to pull it gently shut.

The door stood fast and as she pressed close to it, the cold became unbearable.

A laugh interrupted her thoughts, distant and familiar, the sound of footsteps growing again. They slammed against the floor above her head loudly, as though in some kind of dance. Music began to play, the sound of piano keys and a fiddle playing in tandem, as people cheered and clapped. Bathsheba

All Is Bright

turned towards the noise and as she faced the staircase, she saw a soft light glowing and streaming down from the top floor.

The stubborn door forgotten, Bathsheba quickly ran back to the fire, which roared large and white but gave no heat. She grabbed the cast iron poker, brandishing it like a weapon before she began to slowly ascend the stairs.

The light streamed in from the ballroom, which she had not even bothered to clear out or uncover—except for the deep green chest that rested near the far corner. Bathsheba felt an aura of warmth coming from the room, smelled sweet treats, and caught the movement of shadows as figures moved across the floor and stretched across the wall. They were dancing and making merry, unaware of the intrusion they were committing in her own home. She could swear she heard the crooning voice of old Mistress Mason, speaking harshly of the gravedigger, Gabriel Grubb, and his fierce beating by the goblins on Christmas Eve night. Her Uncle Isaac had told her the same story when she was just a girl on the Christmas Eves before he went away and she never saw him again.

The memory allowed something sharp to settle in the pit of her being. Without further hesitation, Bathsheba marched into the grand room, fire poker brandished. With a quick roar she proclaimed, "Be gone!" but the moment she entered the room, all signs of life disappeared. She was submerged in total darkness, save for the stream of moonlight that poured through the window. It fell upon where a Christmas tree should have sat, and, as if to mourn its memory, it cast a similar shadow onto the empty wall. Beside the shadow rested the deep green chest.

Bathsheba felt as though she were going mad, and she glared in agony at the shadow and the chest locked to her, her throat tight and her mind heavy as it began to pound. She could not bear to keep her eyes open for the pain behind them. The smell of shortbread still lingered in the air and it made her stomach heave as her hands began to shake, her grip on the poker growing weaker as she fought to stay on her feet. The room was colder than the hand of death.

"It is not real," she whispered to the room. It made no response. This time, she screamed. "It is not real!"

Bathsheba heard the door slam downstairs. She dropped the poker and collapsed to the ground, hands resting flat against the chilled hardwood. Her arms shook and she struggled to hold back sobs as she heard heavy footfalls once more ascending the stairs. A deep voice was humming something, but Bathsheba refused to open her eyes. Her knees ached and her teeth chattered. Her entire body was near frozen from the chill and the fear that threatened to stop her young heart.

The footsteps grew louder and the voice clearer. No longer an indistinct hum, it was a deep, rich voice, belonging to a man. As all the voices before it had done, it sang out passionately, "O Come, All Ye Faithful" with a vigour that sought to mock and torment poor Bathsheba's fragile frame.

The steps fell to the entrance of the room and Bathsheba still would not open her eyes to take in whatever fate had in store for her. The voice was loud, distinct now, and so familiar that it halted Bathsheba's breath, a plea for forgiveness fighting to push past her frozen lips and make themselves known. She could not utter a sound.

The footsteps approached, and though she said nothing, her body spoke for her as the floorboards beneath her creaked and groaned as she continued to shake and shiver, her body buzzing like a bee in the blossoming spring. The steps halted just in front of her and she could not stop her body jerking as a cool breeze passed over her. The voice quieted itself now, hardly above a whisper, but it echoed in her ears and bounced within the walls of her mind.

The floorboards before her creaked, as though something sunk to its knees. She felt two gentle hands grasp her shoulders, pulling her away from the floor until she was seated upright on her own knees, too frightened to fight back. The voice stopped singing and Bathsheba felt a cool breath fan across her face, stained with tears she was not aware she had allowed to fall.

All Is Bright

The room began to smell of fresh pine wood, cigar smoke and freshly peeled oranges. Her bottom lip trembled and she felt a soft thumb stroke across it. The clock struck the hour with the first chime of the bell.

"Sweet child," the voice whispered. "Will you not remember me as I was?" it asked. Bathsheba did not open her eyes, yet she knew the sadness that was written across the other's face. The second chime echoed across the room.

"You left me," she answered. "You brought me here to be alone."

"No. Do you not see? I am here, Bathsheba. I am always with you. I never forgot you." A pause fell between, heavy with promise. "You were always in my heart." The third bell chimed.

Bathsheba awoke to the third chime of the bell at eight o'clock on Christmas morning. Her blanket was still wrapped around her shoulders and she was seated in the same plush chair in the drawing room as she had remembered sitting in before dozing off. She rose quickly, ignoring the bristling cold of her feet, and marched to the front door. The latch was closed and the lock turned into its place, just as she had set it before retiring for the night. Turning around, she eyed the staircase with suspicion, before taking off and bounding up them with a singular determination. Everything in the ballroom was as it should seem. All the furniture still covered, no evidence of any party goers or shadows across the wall.

No, the only oddity that remained, was the cast iron fire poker, which rested in the middle of the floor, as though it had always been there.

Mrs. Maise (formally Miss Hollin), was unused to working Christmas Day, but today was a special circumstance. She had been waiting many years to deliver the last letter Isaac Stubbs had bestowed upon her, and his instructions had been quite specific: to deliver the letter and its contents to his niece on the first Christmas morning she spent in the town of Burwick.

She approached the door of Carter Manor, raised her small hand to grasp the large golden knocker, and knocked three times. She waited, listening for the quiet new mistress of the home to answer.

Bathsheba Stubbs answered the door in a state of disarray, her braided hair half fallen out, feet bare, nightgown hanging off one shoulder. Her face was flushed and tear stained. She looked nearly frightened as she took in Mrs. Maise's visage, only seeming to relax after gazing upon her for a moment or two.

"Merry Christmas, Miss Stubbs!" Mrs. Maise cheered happily. "I know this is a bit uncommon, but I have a letter for you. From your uncle. Been holding onto it for some time, but his note was quite specific about not giving it to you until your first Christmas." She held out the letter, yellowed with age and stained with the black ink of Isaac Stubbs' hand. Bathsheba took it carefully, holding it before her as though it were something precious. Mrs. Maise smiled.

"Thank you, Mrs. Maise. I will see you at church."

"You're welcome, Miss Stubbs."

"Merry Christmas," Bathsheba uttered for the first time in many years. Mrs. Maise offered a small wave as she began to walk away and Bathsheba shut the door behind her.

Bathsheba tore into the envelope, which only contained a single piece of paper and a small key. In her uncle's familiar script it read The Green Chest.

Bathsheba ran up the stairs as fast as her shaking legs could carry her, turning into the ballroom and almost tripping over the iron poker which still rested mockingly on the floor. Her vision was blurry and her hands shook as she pulled out the small key, kneeling down in front of the chest and trying to align it with the lock. She had to hold her wrist steady until finally it slid in. With one quick turn to the right, the locks popped open, dust coughing out into the air.

Inside the box rested nearly twenty years' worth of toys, all hand carved, intricate and beautiful. Ballerinas, pirates, boats and trains, a small cat and a large dog and so many other delights all carved from fine wood and painted with delicate

All Is Bright

details, the colours still bright. She pulled each one out and gazed in wonder, noting the unique and familiar work of her uncle's hand in each knot and curve. Beneath the stack of toys was a pile of letters, each with her name and the year written in the top right corner. There was a letter for each and every year since the time her uncle had moved away. At the top rested the one from the year he died. Bathsheba tore into it quickly, and, as he was famous for, found nothing more than a short message written in an elegant, kind and confident hand.

To My Dearest Niece, Bathsheba,

I tried to send some of these toys for many years, but your father always sent them back. I should have come back to you and explained it properly, but we adults do foolish things to protect ourselves and do not often think of those we hurt until it is too late. It is my deepest regret that I did not see you grow older and wiser than I could ever possibly be. If I must leave you with one last thought of me, it is this: I may have left, but you were always in my heart. Enjoy these toys, which are rightfully yours, and read my words which should have been spoken a long time ago. Find comfort in my home and my traditions. Remember me for who I was when I was with you and do not think of me as being gone. I am always with you and I love you across every great distance.

My Deepest Regrets, My Eternal Love, and My Hope for your Happy Future.

I love and miss you.
Uncle Isaac

There is not much to say beyond a simple fact: Bathsheba Stubbs, upon reading the letter, clutched it to her chest and wept. Her cheeks were stained and soaked and her chest ached as she choked and coughed past sobs. Her head pounded and her muscles ached, but she could not help the smile that

All Is Bright

crossed her face.

She spent the hours until church poring over every letter with reverence, care and above all else, love.

When the time had come and Bathsheba had arrived for church, no one in the town of Burwick could tell one another what had changed about Bathsheba Stubbs, but they could all agree that they noticed that something had changed. She still held the same demeanor and her voice still echoed above all the rest, but one could argue that she seemed to sing the hymns with a touch more inflection than she had in the previous masses. Mrs. Maise, known since she was a girl for her love of gossip, had planned to tell the town of the letter she had delivered, but for one reason or another, felt compelled for the first time in her life to keep such business to herself.

The year passed. Bathsheba hired more young men so she could expand the cabinetry business and she improved her skills so she could make more detailed toys. She took on a few of the local girls and taught them how to make dresses. She helped where she could when the annual harvest was due and even began a courtship with one of the local lads just at the beginning of November. Despite how she grew as a member of the community, as December came again, the townsfolk could not help but let their disappointment show at the prospect of another year passing by with no Christmas Eve at Carter Manor and no Isaac Stubbs.

Or so they believed.

The Sunday before Christmas Eve, Bathsheba Stubbs did not show up to morning mass. The Reverend Thomas emerged to stand at his podium, positively beaming, the joy he exuded most unbecoming of a man of God, but no less infectious. The congregation waited anxiously to be addressed.

"I come with the happiest of tidings. A letter from Miss Bathsheba Stubbs for the whole community." Reverend Thomas brandished the letter, which read so:

My dear friends,

All Is Bright

I do hope you shall excuse my rudeness for both not attending mass this morning and for halting, what I have only recently learned, was a beloved tradition in this community. It was wrong of me to stop what my uncle had dedicated so lovingly to his community. Being welcomed in by you has taught me why such kindness deserves such a just and fitting reward. Therefore, I would like to invite everyone in the community, in my uncle's name, to spend Christmas Eve at Carter Manor, where we shall welcome the Lord's son and celebrate together. All those that come with love in their heart are welcome.

May it be the first of many to come.

Yours,
Bathsheba Stubbs

The whole town nearly erupted at the news, the entire congregation cheering as the children bounced around excitedly. Men and women alike began making lists of all they would need in order to prepare. Reverend Thomas gazed down upon his congregation with love and, to himself, sent a silent prayer of thanks to both the Lord Almighty and to Isaac Stubbs.

When Christmas Eve arrived the entire community sat waiting at the church, making sure they had every last man, woman and child before they began their walk. They brought many gifts: wine and cider, delightful treats and hearty, heavy meals. The display was enough to make one's stomach and heart full. Old Mistress Mason was already preparing her storytelling voice and Reverend Thomas had already marked the passage in his bible he would read when the clock struck midnight, the first minute of Christmas Day.

All settled, the town of Burwick began the familiar walk, this time with renewed excitement and gratefulness in their hearts. Without hesitation, they began to sing. They knew they were close to their destination when, as they were singing "O Come, All Ye Faithful," they saw a door open in the distance

All Is Bright

and heard a voice, clear as a bell, join them in their joyous song.

It was a Christmas Eve to remember and the first of many to be hosted by the beautiful Bathsheba Stubbs. She would grow to be quite the influential woman, eventually marrying and raising two beautiful girls, to whom she taught her many skills and her renewed love of Christmas. Their voices, too, rang louder than any others in the whole of the congregation.

And no one, save for you and I, ever learned the full truth for the reason behind Bathsheba's transformation, but they suspected that Isaac Stubbs had something to do with it. The emerald green chest, which had always been closed, now sat open each Christmas Eve and the town's small children all shared in the joy of the toys that Isaac Stubbs had crafted with love and reverence. Each year, Bathsheba herself added a new toy to the collection, carrying on her uncle's legacy. And for those that remembered him, Isaac Stubbs was always seen— not just in the room, so filled with celebration, but in his niece's warm eyes as she took in the sight of all he had created and all she had given back.

It soon became known throughout the town of Burwick that Bathsheba Stubbs and Christmas were one and the same, and those who were children when she hosted her first Christmas soon grew old enough to bring their own children. It was always a wonderful night, filled with joy, laughter, and love.

May that be said truly of the Christmas Eves we all share, and may we never forget the traditions and people we love. May we always welcome those that come with love in their hearts to share in the home we have made together.

The End

About the Author

N.A. Kimber is a 23-year-old writer from Caledon, Ontario. She has been writing for twelve years as a means of exploring different worlds and voices and has always been moved by the power of storytelling across all mediums. Kimber is constantly seeking to broaden her horizons as a writer while working to publish and promote her own work. She has practice in several genres of writing, ranging from novels and short stories to poetry and scripts. She is always looking for new challenges, themes or methods to apply to her own work. Kimber particularly enjoys writing pieces that either encourage self-reflection or questioning, or pieces that challenge and bring her out of her comfort zone while connecting honestly with herself and the world around her.

The Magic of Christmastime

by Sue Magby

The magic of Christmastime comes once a year,
with carolers singing and lots of good cheer.

It starts in our heart but must never stay there—
the spirit of Christmas was given to share.

True joy is not found in the baubles and things,
the wrappings and trappings that stores try to bring,

but rather in serving and letting light shine.
In each little story, see love that's divine:

The sweet little girl and her family so poor,
they live in a house that has dirt for the floor.

She saves all the pennies she finds in the streets
to buy her dear friend a small Christmas day treat.

A father who's jobless now fights back the tears—
There's nothing to place 'neath the tree is his fear.

All Is Bright

Then Twelve Days of Christmas are secretly done
to bring them all joy and some seasonal fun.

There's one who's abandoned by those he calls kin.
He lives in a shack and his wallet is thin.

But go search for him at this holiday time,
and he will be feeding the homeless in line.

This holiday season, let love be a part,
The giving comes easy—you'll see once you start!

So do what you can to give someone a lift—
yes, acts from the heart are the very best gift.

Just think if we did this throughout the whole year…
then Christmastime magic would always be here!

About the Author

Sue Magleby adores children and believes each has divine worth and potential. She feels reading a book to a child unlocks their world, sets their imagination free and shows them they are worthy of our time.

Growing up an only daughter in the backwoods of New Hampshire, she spent many hours alone, but not lonely. Her menagerie of stuffed animals not only kept her company but was always there with a listening ear for her imaginative stories and short poems.

Sue studied elementary education and has taught preschool and kindergarten. She currently volunteers at a local elementary school as a reading tutor. She is also a member of SCBWI.

Having raised her three children, she is now enjoying her four grandchildren. Following her personal motto, "She believed she could, so she did," Sue has started writing her own children's picture books in hopes they will someday amuse, inspire and invoke a love for reading in others.

To Hope and to Dance

By Adrienne Powell

Eleven-year-old Laynie Edwards stood in the middle of the room, squinting her eyes in concentration as she slid her foot across the floor in a tendu.

"Turn out, turn out!" Miss Angela said. "Lead with your heel."

Laynie pushed her heel forward and reminded her toes to stay pointed and her arms to relax and her stomach to stay in and her fingers to be energetic. That was all her brain could hold at once.

In the mirror, a dozen other girls were concentrating just as hard. Well, almost as hard. No one concentrated as hard as Laynie.

After class was over, she climbed in the car with her mom. At first she seemed a little quieter than usual, but soon she asked, "How was class?"

"Good. We're starting to learn entrechats."

"What is that?"

"It's the kind of jump where you switch your legs back and forth in the air before you land."

All Is Bright

"How exciting! You'll have to show me when we get home."

After a few minutes, her mom spoke again. "Laynie, you know how Dad has been feeling worse over the last few months?"

"Yeah?" Her dad's health had been going downhill for some time, but now it was getting bad enough that it was hard for him to do normal, everyday things.

"Dad might have to stop going to work for a while."

"Oh. Do we have enough money?"

"We don't know how long this will last. We think there will be enough to live on for a while, but we don't know about dance."

"What?" Laynie bit her lip, trying to stop the lump that had just formed in her throat.

"I'm sorry, honey. I know how much you love it. If Dad gets better we might be able to get you back into it next year, but right now I just can't see how it will work."

"Can I finish the semester at least?"

"Yes, we've already paid for this whole semester. We won't take you out until January."

Laynie sat in silence for a moment, trying to hold back the tears that were squeezing their way out of her eyes. "Mom, I won't get to be in the spring recital. We just got to see pictures of our costumes today. We were going to wear real tutus." Now her nose was starting to run.

Laynie's mom pulled into the driveway and put her arm around her. "I'm really sorry."

That night, Laynie prayed the same thing she always did: "Please help Daddy get better." And then she added, "Please, please help Daddy get better so we can have enough money. You know how to do miracles, right? Can you please make a miracle so I can keep dancing?"

Later that week as she practiced her pliés, an idea burst into Laynie's mind. Maybe she could pay for her own dance classes.

All Is Bright

If she worked as hard making money as she did while dancing, then maybe she could earn enough.

"Turn out, Laynie!" Miss Angela called.

Laynie tried to focus on turning out her feet, but it was hard with the idea bouncing itself around her head like petit allegro. It wasn't any easier as class wore on to remember to spot her pirouettes or plié between her sautés.

She burst into the car as soon as class was over and announced, "Mom, I'm going to try to earn lots of money and pay for my dance classes. Do you know how I can earn money?"

"Laynie, I think that's a wonderful idea. I'm going to try to get a part-time job that I can do at home. Maybe you can babysit Lucas while I work?"

So Laynie learned to cook and change diapers and how to feed the baby and rock him to sleep. It was much more tiring than she had expected, especially after long days of school and dance class, but she kept reminding herself, It's for ballet. It's so I can keep dancing. And when baby Lucas was fussy or hard to handle, that thought gave her just enough energy to go on.

October faded into November and Laynie kept trying. After a bit of math she realized that if she kept going at the rate she was, then by Christmas she would have enough money for one month of lessons. But tuition for the whole semester was due on January first. She needed to make a lot more money to be ready in time.

Laynie thought and thought. Maybe some of the neighbors would let her watch their pets while they were on vacation.

The next day, Laynie walked around the neighborhood and knocked on every door. "Hi, are you going somewhere for Thanksgiving? Do you need someone to watch your pet?"

One person after another said they weren't going anywhere, they didn't have a pet, someone was already watching their cat. Laynie walked more and more slowly. The cold wind was not lifting her spirits. Snow started to swirl, but it danced cold and hard like the Snow Queen's minions, not soft and elegant like

All Is Bright

the waltzing flurries in The Nutcracker. After the last house Laynie turned around and went home.

She kicked off her boots and plopped onto the couch. "It's no use, Ryan," she said to her little brother. "How does a kid make four hundred dollars?"

Ryan shrugged. "Sell stuff?"

"Like what?"

"I don't know. Lemonade?"

"Ryan, it's cold outside."

He shrugged again and went back to building his train set.

Laynie thought some more. Ryan did have a point. Selling things was a good idea, but what in the world could an eleven-year-old sell? She trooped down to her parents' room where her dad was resting on the bed.

"Hey Dad, what can I sell to make money for dance?"

"Hmm..." He thought for a long moment, almost seeming to forget what he had been asked. Then he roused himself and said, "Maybe hot chocolate?"

Laynie's face perked up. "Yeah! Can you help me?"

"If you make the hot chocolate and sit outside with it, then I can help make the sign and set things up."

"Yay!" She was bouncing on the bed now. "Can we start right now?"

"Give me fifteen more minutes to rest."

The next day after school, Laynie hurried to set up her table and heat the hot chocolate. She put up the sign and set out the cups. Then she sat and waited.

Soon, customers started to trickle in. People on the street pulled over to get some and a few neighbors dropped by. When the supply of hot chocolate had run out, Laynie had made seventeen dollars.

The weeks rolled on, Thanksgiving passed, the Snow Queen performance approached, and rehearsals grew more frequent. Laynie kept her hot chocolate stand going every

All Is Bright

week. She bundled up against the cold and worked on her homework in between customers. By now she was exhausted. She looked forward to Christmas break, when there would be more time and no homework.

"Please, God," Laynie prayed. "I'm out of ideas. Please help me be able to dance next semester. I don't even have to get Christmas presents. I just want to dance. Please help me get enough money."

One day after class Miss Angela came up to Laynie and reminded her that costume fees were due for the spring recital.

"I don't think I can do it," Laynie mumbled, not making eye contact. She had been holding onto hope for so long, but now it seemed too late.

"How come?"

Laynie went red. "I don't have enough money. I might not be able to dance next semester."

Miss Angela bent down and gave her a hug. "I'm really sorry, Laynie. I can tell that ballet means a lot to you, so this must be very hard. We'll really miss you if you can't come back."

Christmas came with all its lights and smells, and Laynie had only enough money for two months' tuition. Early in the morning she crept downstairs. As she had expected, Santa Claus hadn't brought a lot of presents. There were a few from her grandparents, one from her parents, and a large package Laynie didn't recognize. She opened that one first.

As soon as the wrapping paper was peeled off, Laynie gasped. Inside was a dark blue tutu with gold and silver brocade on the bodice and gilding the edges. It was even more beautiful than in the pictures. With it was a note from Miss Angela that said, Merry Christmas, Laynie! I love teaching you and watching you work so hard. I know how much you love to dance, and I hope you will enjoy this costume.

Laynie hugged the tutu to herself, twirled around, tried it on, and twirled some more. Then her face fell. "But I won't get

All Is Bright

to wear it."

"Open your other presents," her mom said.

Laynie opened the one from her parents next. Her jaw dropped. It was a coupon made of cardstock that said, Good for one half of a semester of ballet. Love, Mom and Dad.

Laynie looked up at her parents with her mouth still wide open. Mom smiled. "You've been working really hard, Laynie. With the money you've earned, and the way you've helped me, I think there will be enough for you to finish the year."

Laynie curled up between her parents, too amazed to speak.

Five months later, Laynie pulled her hair into a tight, sprayed bun, put on the brightest makeup she had, climbed into her blue tutu, and lined up in the wings with her classmates. Blinding lights came up and Mozart began to play. Twelve small ballerinas walked onstage and began to dance. Laynie twirled and lept, turned and soared, and she felt alive.

When the music ended and Laynie took her final curtsy, she whispered, "Thank you, God."

About the Author

Adrienne Powell has been writing since she was small and dancing since she was even smaller. She loves all things creative and outdoors. Adrienne is from West Virginia but is currently studying linguistics at Brigham Young University. Her first work, an essay titled *Broken,* was published in August 2020.

The Christmas Dollar

By Jim Roberts

It was a few days before Christmas and the man sat silently in an old wooden rocking chair, staring down at his hands. They trembled as he rocked slowly back and forth with his eyes fixated on the dollar bill between his aged and wrinkled fingers. This was not simply any dollar bill—it was his final one.

The road had been rough at times, but they had always seemed to make it through so long as they were together. They had been together 57 years when she simply did not wake up one morning. The angels had come and taken her in the night, and that left him all alone since they had never been blessed with kids of their own.

Sounds of the clock ticking on the wall echoed in the small living room in harmony with the creaking of the rocking chair. With the loneliness almost too much to take, an idea started to take shape. It began more like a snowball than an avalanche, but as it grew a smile started to show itself behind the long white whiskers of the old man's face.

What's in a dollar? he thought.

Out he went into the winter cold to find the Christmas spirit that was lacking this year with his dollar bill stuffed deep into the empty pocket of his trousers. He had to use

All Is Bright

suspenders to keep his pants from falling down because a belt simply would not work with his pot belly physique. With his winter jacket on and suspenders locked in tight, he started a slow walk through the snow.

It was not long before he had to take a break and catch his breath. Clouds of smoke seemed to come out his mouth with each exhale as he scanned the scene before him, hoping, praying even, that he could capture what his heart so desperately longed for. His gaze stopped as he saw a bundle of a person leaning against a nearby building, trying their best to stay warm in the frigid temperatures. A thought crossed his mind: *I bet that person needs this dollar more than I do!*

Off he went to give away the last dollar of the month in hopes Christmas magic would return. He removed the wool mitten from his right hand and dug into his pocket to find the crumpled bill. As he approached the man leaning on the building, the old man extended his arm to shake the hand of the stranger.

"Merry Christmas!" he exclaimed as he seamlessly transferred the bill from his hand to the hand of this new found friend.

All the old man could see were eyes peeking out from behind the scarf and beanie that were doing their best to cover the person's entire face. As the old man gave a smile and saw a twinkle in the eye of the stranger he looked down to see what was in the palm of his hand.

"Hey mister. Merry Christmas to you! Are you sure you don't need this hundred dollar bill?" the stranger asked.

"What are you talking about?" the old man said. "I simply thought you could use the dollar to buy a cup of hot chocolate to keep you warm."

"Well, this will buy me lots of cups of cocoa, but this also gives me just enough to get the ticket to see my family. It's kinda like a miracle. You just made my Christmas wish come true!"

As the scarf slipped from the stranger's face, the old

All Is Bright

man could see he was young, probably a college student. The stranger's eyes were filled with the same Christmas light the old man remembered in his wife's eyes. As he turned to walk away he muttered to himself, "A Christmas miracle indeed. Merry Christmas."

Confused was an understatement. What just happened? He knew it was a dollar bill, not a hundred. Those were few and far between in his house. His eyesight was starting to fade, which was why he wore the half-lensed glasses near the tip of his nose, but he knew for sure he did not miss two zeros on that bill. His mind was still as sharp as ever, so he was confident in what he knew, but this little experience had him questioning his sanity. He rubbed his white beard, trying to grasp what had just happened. Maybe that hundred dollar bill had been in his pocket the entire time, he kept telling himself unconvincingly.

Slowly, almost out of a sense of fear, he slid his hand into the right pocket of his trousers and dug deep to see what he could find. There, at the bottom of the pocket, he felt it. His heart skipped a beat because he knew that feeling. To his fingertips it was the unmistakable feel of a bill. He pulled it out to see his wrinkled dollar bill. His last dollar bill, he quickly recalled. He concluded he must have had the other bill in his pocket already, but to be safe, he checked both pockets to confirm there were no more surprises.

Feeling confident all that was left was his original dollar, he started his shuffle down the sidewalk in search of someone else who needed that dollar more than he did. He still could not wrap his mind around what had just happened. He was so sure all he had was just a dollar.

Off in the distance he heard the sounds of jingle bells and children laughing. He knew that was where he needed to go to feel the Christmas spirit. As he walked, the old man's cheeks started to turn red from the cold and this made them stand out next to his bright white beard. Again, the thought came to him, *It is only a dollar.*

The one thing the old man could not deny was that he

All Is Bright

could not wipe the smile from his face, and he had forgotten how lonely he had felt. He paused to watch kids slide down the sled hill, squealing with delight as their mothers looked on. He turned as he heard the sound of jingle bells beside him. Next to him stood a mother with small little jingle bells attached to her boots so her kids would know where she was when she walked. It was as if it was her simple way to spread Christmas cheer. His smile broadened as the memory came to him that his wife used to do the same thing each and every Christmas season.

"Mom!" yelled a little boy as he came running toward her. "Did you see me jump the snowbank on my sled, Mom? Did you see me? Did you see how high I got? Did you see me crash? Mom, I didn't even cry. Mom, did you see me?"

"Yes, Tommy, I saw you. You went so high and I am so proud of you," the mother replied.

The old man decided to make this young man's day by giving him his dollar. *What kid does not love a dollar?* he thought to himself. He once again removed his wool mitten and plunged into his pocket. His mouth formed an "O" and his eyebrows came together as he pulled out a shiny, new matchbox car.

"Excuse me, son, I have a little gift for you if it is okay with your mother," the old man began as he held out the car in his hand for the boy and his mom to see.

"MOM, That's the same car I lost at Austin's house. I have not been able to find it anywhere after we played in the mud. It is my favorite car, mom. Pleeeeeeeeeease!" pleaded the boy.

"How did you know?" asked the mom. "I mean, it seems miraculous that of all the cars you would offer my son, you would give him the car that he lost? I have been looking all over town and even online for that exact car, and I have not been able to find it anywhere. He told me last night that all he wanted for Christmas was to find his favorite car. I don't know how I can thank you enough."

"It really is my pleasure, miss. I think it's more of a miracle to me than to you, if you can believe it. Merry Christmas!" he said as he turned and walked away, shaking his head.

He decided to check his pocket once again, and out he pulled his dollar bill with a little bit of lint, but that was it. Nothing else filled his pockets, but his mind was racing trying to piece together this mysterious puzzle. He could feel his heart being filled with the Christmas spirit, and he was now both anxious and excited to try and give away his dollar yet again, unsure what may actually happen.

With his head down and lost in thought, he walked for what seemed like hours, but it was merely a few minutes when his head snapped up at the sound of a horn honking loudly. He turned to see a truck heading right for him as he realized he was standing in the middle of the crosswalk. By accident he'd failed to catch the solid red hand instructing him not to walk. With the roads being snow-packed, the truck had no chance of stopping before impact, and the old man stood frozen in the truck's path. A moment before he expected to be struck by the truck, he was knocked over from the side by a blur and slid to a stop just outside the reach of the truck's oversized tires.

Slowly the old man rose to his feet and dusted the snow from his clothes. He turned and looked down to see a white and orange dog standing expectantly with his stub of a tail wagging eagerly as if he was waiting for a treat. Was this the blur that hit him from the side, he wondered silently?

Seeing a pedestrian on the other side of the street, the old man yelled out, "Did you see what just happened?"

The witness explained the dog came out of nowhere and knocked him over and out of the way just before the truck was going to hit him. The old man could not believe what he was hearing. He had been lost in thought and had haphazardly walked into the intersection in front of a truck, and he was saved by a dog? Was he dreaming?

"RUSTY! Rusty, come here boy!" a man yelled as he came around the corner toward the old man and the dog.

"I am so sorry, sir!" the man exclaimed. "This is my dog, Rusty, and he runs off sometimes. I sure hope he was not

All Is Bright

bothering you too much. He loves people, but sometimes he loves them a little too much and has a terrible habit of jumping up on people he likes."

"Did you see what just happened?" inquired the old man.

"No I didn't. He got away from me and I lost sight of him when he went around the corner. Please don't tell me he knocked you down?"

"Well, he did knock me down, as a matter of fact," the old man began. He saw the man's facial expression start to sag so he quickly continued, "But in doing so he actually saved my life! A Christmas miracle is what I would call it."

The old man went on to explain how the dog had knocked him out of the way of the oncoming truck.

He was pretty sure at this point he was not dreaming, even though he could not explain the recent series of events. He could feel the pounding in his elbow from where he struck the ground, so he figured he did not need to pinch himself to make sure he was awake. He remembered the dollar in his pocket and told the man, "I would like to give you something for saving my life. I don't have much, but I want you to have it as a token of my gratitude."

The man kindly refused as he clipped the leash onto his dog's collar. "I don't need anything at all. I am just glad you were not injured and that both you and Rusty are safe."

"I insist, and I won't take no for an answer."

The old man dug into his pocket once again, and this time he was not as surprised to feel something other than a dollar bill. He felt something that seemed like a small box, even though he knew beyond all doubt his pocket only contained that solitary dollar bill. He slowly drew out his hand and let out an audible gasp when he saw the jewelry box resting in his hand.

"This, my boy, is for you."

"Sir, I cannot take this. I'm sure you bought it for your wife or daughter, and you need to give it to one of them. It's not mine to take, but I appreciate your offer."

All Is Bright

The old man looked through his ice-blue eyes into the soul of the man standing before him. He felt the warmth of a tear trickling down his cheek. This was not a tear of sadness, for his heart was full. It was a tear of gratitude. He did not know what happened to his dollar, but he knew deep down this little box with a treasure inside belonged to the man standing before him.

"Has anyone ever said you look a lot like Santa?"

With his rosy cheeks, white beard, round belly, blue eyes, and half glasses, it was a wonder more people did not ask him the same exact question.

"No, son. I am not Santa. I am just an old man looking for a little Christmas spirit. I've found that giving what I have is the best way to find it. All I know for sure is that this little box is for you, so please accept this gift as a token of my gratitude since your pup saved my life."

The man gently took the box from the old man and opened it up to find a simple, yet elegant, diamond ring. This time the tears started streaming from the man with the dog. He could not take his eyes off the ring inside the box. He struggled to contain the emotions.

"Oh my! It is beautiful. What are you going to do with it?" the old man inquired as his thoughts wandered back in time to the moment he opened a similar box for his bride-to-be over 57 years ago. The smile across his face could not be contained as the memories flooded back.

"You have no idea what this means to me. I have been saving and saving, but I never seem to get ahead these days. Sarah always says she doesn't need a ring as a sign of our love, but I have been trying so hard to get her one. This is the best Christmas present I could give her. How did you know it was what I have been working so hard for? If you don't mind, I am going to call you Santa because you just made my Christmas wishes come true."

The old man let out a nice chuckle and affirmed, "You, my son, can call me Santa if you would like. If you are calling me

All Is Bright

Santa, what shall I call you?"

"The name is Sam. You know, Santa, since I don't see any sleigh or reindeer around, can I give you a lift somewhere? Rusty and I were out doing some window shopping when he got away from me, and I'm parked just around the corner."

The old man thought about how tired he was feeling and how long it would take him to mosey back to his cozy home, so he accepted the offer with a simple, "That would be nice."

Each man was lost in his thoughts on the ride back to "Santa's" place, so all was quiet except for Rusty barking at each passerby. He seemed to want to play with everyone as he bounced from side to side, keeping the slobber flowing on each of the back seat windows.

The car slowly rolled to a stop outside the old man's snow-covered picket fence. He wished Sam and his fur ball a final Merry Christmas and made his way to the front door. His mind spun from all that had happened since he left that morning. Unexplainable was the best way to explain his day.

He gently closed the door and leaned back against it with flashbacks of his day. He thought of the loneliness he felt at the beginning and then progressed through the events that transpired. The eyes of the college student longing to get home for the holiday reminded him of his wife's eyes and the joy of Christmas. Ringing jingle bells on the boots of the mother flooded his mind with the beautiful memories of all the things his wife would do to usher in Christmas cheer. Then, who could forget the ring that so closely resembled the one he had given his wife so many years ago? As he reflected on the day's events, he realized his wife was everywhere he went. Suddenly, he did not feel alone at all. He felt her presence all around him, and his heart was more full of love and of the Christmas spirit than he could ever remember before.

He decided to take off his coat and drape it on the hanger next to the door as he beamed with gratitude for the day's events. Next, he slipped off his big, black boots and was just about ready to go find his spot in his rocking chair when

All Is Bright

he remembered his last dollar. With joyful thoughts of the miracles that followed his dollar, he gently dug into his pocket one last time. Since no one else was around, he was startled to feel something hard instead of the wadded up bill. His heart started racing, and he was thinking he ought to sit down. He had no idea what could be in his pocket this time. Ever so slowly his fingers wrapped around this foreign object. He could not tell what it was based on feeling alone. He removed it from his pocket and peered through his half glasses at the final Christmas miracle.

Through his spectacles the item became clear. He instantly knew that this object was just for him. Each gift he had given that day was specific to the receiver, and he knew this gift was his. Carefully, he cradled the object in both hands and peered down in adoration. Resting in his weathered hands was a small figurine of a baby lying in a manger. Light seemed to emanate from the small figure as he gazed upon it.

In an instant it was as if the day became clear, and in a strange sort of way it all made sense. He was not sure how it happened, he just understood why. He remembered the Christmas spirit was the spirit of giving. He felt love radiating from his core, and he knew without a doubt he would not be alone that Christmas. He knew he was loved, not alone. He knew that somehow, and for some reason, he provided what a few others needed to fill their hearts with the Christmas spirit. His beard looked a little whiter that day. His belly a little rounder, cheeks a little rosier, and his boots a little shinier. As he pulled his trusty old rocker up to the fire, he could feel a little something else in his pocket. Before sitting down to rest, he dug deep into the recesses of his trousers and removed his Christmas dollar. Ever so carefully, he placed it on the mantle next to the manger that held the greatest gift of all.

About the Author

Jim Roberts grew up in the rural cowboy town of Camp Verde in central Arizona. The open space and lack of other kids in the neighborhood other than his younger brother fostered the need for creativity. He obtained a BS in Chemistry from Southern Utah University, and he puts the degree to good use each and every day as an owner of an Arizona-based mortgage company. In his free time between running 4 kids around the state for sporting events and service with his church, he enjoys time at the family cabin and going on runs with the two family dogs, where he finds himself questioning his sanity for strapping two pups to his waist when they only know break-neck speed.

Gingersnap Glee

By Anabella Schofield

Snowfall descended into the valley and glimmered in the light of the chilly winter sky. I shivered and exhaled in awe, captivated by the scene.

I blinked. My imagination had taken me to a winter wonderland of my own. In reality, an avalanche of sugar had cascaded from a crinkly bag into a valley—no, bowl—constructed of ceramic. No snow would fall upon our warm and bright California home, especially not in our cozy kitchen.

My mother smiled down at me as I wiped my hands on my checkered apron and lunged for a spatula. Along with my sister, who wore an identical apron, my mom and I were fulfilling our Christmas tradition of making gingersnaps.

I gripped the pale yellow mixing bowl—the very one my grandma had used to make cookies—and stirred the ingredients with an unskilled hand until the dough was uniform and smooth.

"Ready to make some snowballs?" asked my mom, her eyes twinkling.

"Yes, please!" I beamed. I slid the bowl across the table to my mom, who expertly shaped the caramel-colored dough

All Is Bright

into spheres. Sofia and I took turns rolling each ball of ginger-molasses in the bowl of sugar, coating them in an extra layer of sweetness.

My mom put the gingersnaps in the oven, and soon the aroma of cinnamon and sugar floated through the kitchen. For a moment, I dreamed I was living in a gingerbread house.

The scent of baking cookies tempted me. But I was not going to eat any of these gingersnaps; they were to be delivered to friends and family, a tradition my generous grandmother had established. Though my sister and I were born after my grandma had left the earth, I felt closest to her when serving others.

The timer announced that the cookies had finally finished baking. After the cookies cooled, I smiled as I arranged them on snowflake-patterned plates. My mom enveloped the plates in plastic wrap and my sister placed festive bows and gift tags on each one just as my dad zoomed up our driveway.

"Gingersnaps!" he exclaimed, grinning as he entered the back door, removed his dress shoes, and swung his backpack off his shoulder. "Great work, girls!" He gave us each a squeeze.

Shortly after, we all climbed into my mom's Expedition and arranged towers of gingersnap-filled plates on our laps. I hugged my column of cookies tightly as my dad cruised down roads filled with a galaxy's worth of holiday lights. Sofia and I hummed along to the radio, thrilled to listen to Christmas songs and view sparkling sights.

As we drove to various houses, leaving plates on doorsteps and disappearing after the ring of a doorbell, my family and I exchanged smiles, imagining our loved ones' delight when they opened their doors.

When we arrived home, a warm, spicy fragrance still lingered in the air. I inhaled deeply, smiling with contentment. We had arrived home empty-handed, but my heart was filled with joy. Though I had not partaken of the gingersnaps, giving the cookies was far more satisfying than eating them.

About the Author

Anabella Schofield is the co-author and co-illustrator of *Ladybug's Garden* and *Ladybug's Christmas*. She is enchanted by the art of storytelling through words, music, film, fashion, illustration, photography and hand-lettering. Anabella loves to collaborate with her twin sister, Sofia, and seeks to find and create beauty in the world. She hopes her work uplifts you and brings you a smile.

Spreading the Spirit of Gratitude All Year Long

By Sofia Schofield

Although it was the day after Christmas, carols from my mom's favorite *Alabama Christmas* album resounded throughout the kitchen. My twin sister, Anabella, and I sat together at the table eating lunch, reindeer-emblazoned placemats underneath our plates of leftover ham and homemade rolls. Between us, a carefully-frosted gingerbread house stood proudly, its cookie inhabitants drooping in their attempts to remain standing. Elementary school art projects with popsicle sticks and pipe cleaners galore were scattered across the refrigerator, and our school pictures grinned back at us from inside Christmas-themed frames. A magnetic notepad with Hello Kitty-themed paper clung to the side of the fridge, where the front page displayed a neatly written list in my mother's handwriting. She entered the room, gently ripped the list from the notepad, and placed it in front of us. It read, "People to thank."

"Time to write some thank you notes," she announced with a smile.

We finished eating our meal and cleared up the dishes. I opened the art drawer and pulled out a plastic bag bulging with dozens of colored pencils. Our mom helped us fold a stack of papers into ready-made cards, and we set to work, humming along to the Christmas CD. The first note we wrote was to our grandfather. I inscribed a message thanking him for our new slippers, then slid the card over to Anabella. She wrote "Thank you!" in cursive on the cover, then added an illustration of her fluffy blue slippers alongside my pink ones. We signed our names, and for the final step, I drew the rectangle logo of our homemade card company, "A + S Cards." We checked our grandfather's name off the list, and I selected a new note to illustrate. While Anabella wrote a message inside another card, I created a colored pencil rendering of the stuffed animals we received from our aunt. We continued swapping cards back and forth until the writing and illustrating tasks for each one were accomplished. My mom scooped up the finished stack of cards, placing them inside the envelopes she had already addressed and stamped for us, and with that, our cards were ready to mail. Envisioning smiles spread across my loved ones' faces when they received their notes, I beamed to imagine that our cards could brighten their days.

My sister and I have never known our grandmothers in this life; both of them passed away before we were born. With this knowledge and out of the kindness of their hearts, several wonderful women in my life have acted as fairy godmothers to my sister and me. When one of these friends approached us at church one winter afternoon, I did not expect to hear what she had to say. She leaned on her cane as she told us that she had received a card from us in the mail, thanking her for the Christmas gifts she had so generously given us, and then she made this statement in her gentle, grandmotherly voice:

"You know, I've kept every single one of those notes you've sent me over the years."

I stood there, stunned, for a second. "Really?" I vocalized incredulously, and my sister echoed my surprise. "That is so sweet of you!" I exclaimed, reaching down to give her a hug.

All Is Bright

Even after the encounter, my mind was pleasantly occupied with her kind remark. After years of sending thank you note after thank you note to someone who truly deserved each one, the thought had crossed my mind that perhaps my endeavors to express my appreciation for her had become repetitive, and I wondered if I had adequately thanked her. Yet somehow, she had prized our cards enough to save each one. Each time I recall this experience, I feel grateful that my mom so lovingly encouraged my sister and me to form the habit of thanking others. Even if my expressions of gratitude feel insufficient at times, perhaps my efforts can add up to have a greater impact than I realize.

The Christmas season is a special time to express gratitude. As we strive to remember the Savior, the perfect Gift to the world, we can cultivate gratitude all year long. Jesus Christ shows us how to be grateful in all circumstances. Frequently cited is the story of the ten lepers, as found in Luke 17:11-19, which offers a poignant perspective on the importance of thanking God. When the Savior heals ten individuals suffering from leprosy, nine of them continue onward instead of turning back to thank Him. Jesus questions, "Were there not ten cleansed? but where are the nine?" (Luke 17:17). He then addresses the man who returned to thank Him: "Arise, go thy way: thy faith hath made thee whole." (Luke 17:19). Every time I read about the ten lepers, I think about how I want to be the one who takes the time to turn back in thankfulness. In all that I do to show gratitude to God and to the people in my life, it is my sincere desire to become more like the Savior, who exemplified what it truly means to be grateful.

A Night at San Francisco Ballet's *Nutcracker*

By Sofia Schofield

Rain drums on the roof of my dad's beloved BMW, cascading down the windows and arranging in patterns across the window panes. I watch as a single raindrop collides with droplets in its path, leaving a tiny trail of water down the window until it slides out of sight. Through the fogged-up glass, I gaze at the gleaming city lights as the familiar skyscrapers of San Francisco come into view. The parade of cars inches down the pavement as we battle through traffic, slowly approaching our destination: the War Memorial Opera House. As we drive downtown, the dome of City Hall looms ahead with alternating red-and-green spotlights. Colorful banners on Van Ness Avenue proclaim the showtimes of the San Francisco Ballet *Nutcracker*, complete with portraits of characters from the performance. After turning into a parking garage, we spiral higher and higher in search of an empty spot. We reach the second-highest level of the garage before locating a place to park. Finally, our car comes to rest.

My dad smiles. "Ready, girls?"

"Yes!" my twin sister and I exclaim in unison, eagerly clambering out of the car.

All Is Bright

Opting for the narrow, dimly-lit concrete staircase instead of the rickety elevator, we wind downstairs until we reach ground level, emerging into the chilly city air. Clutching our coats tightly around us, we come to the end of the block and join the crowd on the sidewalk corner right as the pedestrian symbol flashes. Trying not to trip in my high heels, I hold my dad's hand and dash across the crosswalk.

After our tickets are scanned, we are swept inside the Opera House and into a grand lobby. I tilt my head back to admire the gold-adorned ceiling. Calls of "Programs, get your programs!" resound as we pause for a photograph by an elaborate Christmas tree. Our footsteps echo as we make our way up a marble staircase. Ponytail swinging, I skip up a ramp and push open the door that separates us from our seats. A smile spreads across my face as I survey the interior of the theater: an enormous light fixture graces the ceiling and a magnificent gold curtain shields the stage from view. Hundreds of red velvet seats line the room in rows that steadily fill up as audience members take their seats. Locating our assigned aisle, we sink into our own seats and wait for the ballet to begin.

Before we know it, darkness pervades the room, and a wave of the conductor's baton brings Tchaikovsky's iconic composition into existence. The curtain rises to reveal an old-fashioned San Franciscan street. Applause rings throughout the theater for a brief moment, vanishing as excited whispers subside and the familiar Christmas tale comes to life. My awestruck eyes flicker back and forth between the dancers and musicians; I marvel at the skillfully designed sets and sequin-bedazzled costumes, the precision of the dancers, the emotion depicted by the orchestra. I am captivated by the story woven onstage, moved by the flawless artistry before me.

As the ballerina portraying Clara is presented with a toy nutcracker, I open my purse and pull out a miniature replica—a souvenir my dad purchased from a previous year. His eyes twinkle as he notices the toy in my hands. A battle between the Mouse King and the Nutcracker ensues, and a

All Is Bright

cannon is wheeled onstage. I plug my ears in anticipation of the deafening crash that always seems to catch me by surprise. My heart skips as the cannon blast reverberates, enveloping the dancers in smoke. The audience's gasps transform into giggles as the Mouse King places his foot inside a giant mousetrap, dramatically flailing down a trapdoor in defeat.

I glance over at my sister in delight, our identical blue eyes glistening as one of our favorite scenes begins: "The Waltz of the Snowflakes." The ballerinas' pointe shoes pound audibly against the stage with every step as snow descends upon the dancers, falling thickly around them. I watch in awe as the entire stage is coated in a layer of snow; the dancers are barely visible amidst the storm. Clara arrives, her sled carving cleanly through the snow, and the curtain falls for intermission.

Rising from our seats, my sister and I take our father's hands once more, and we wander about the halls of the Opera House together. We stop to admire the city sights through the windows, glance at stuffed animals and snow globes at the gift shop, and rush back to the theater as the bell beckons the audience to return.

The evening's show wears on, and I try not to yawn as the clock ticks closer to my bedtime. I sit up straighter in my seat as the "Pas de Deux" commences, beaming again at my sister. My eyes shine as I witness the sheer beauty of the scene, the dancers' movements combining seamlessly with a passionate cello melody.

As the ballet concludes and each dancer takes a bow, thunderous applause echoes throughout the theater, and the golden curtain falls with finality. We linger until we are the last guests left, watching as the crew hoists set pieces off the stage. With the Sugar Plum Fairy still dancing in our heads, we exit the Opera House and climb the concrete staircase to our car, humming Nutcracker music all the way.

On the ride home, we listen to carols on the radio while recounting our favorite moments from the ballet. We share our wonder at the gifts shared by those who performed, thankful

All Is Bright

to have been uplifted by their talents and dedication. My sister and I enthusiastically express gratitude to our dad for taking us to the ballet—a present that cannot be unwrapped, but is rather recollected—the gift of time spent together at Christmastime and special memories to hold dear to our hearts.

About the Author

Sofia Schofield is the co-author of Ladybug's Garden and Ladybug's Christmas, which she wrote and illustrated with her twin sister, Anabella. Sofia enjoys photography, writing, music, and illustration, and she loves collaborating with her sister on their shared hobbies. Sofia absolutely adores Christmastime, and she is happy to share some of her Christmas memories with you.

A Yellowstone Christmas

By Lori Widdison

Chapter One

Samantha Gentry hummed along to the Christmas tune playing over the shop's speakers as she finished the safety inspection on Axel's car. All the employees except Axel had already left for the day.

"You know, Axle Grease, you're lucky I noticed your oil change was overdue. The oil I just emptied was bordering on dangerous looking. I can't believe you waited this long to get it done." She glared at her young employee. "You should know better."

The tall young man blushed. "I know, I know, boss lady. I've just been a little distracted lately."

"Well, if you don't want your 'distraction'" —Sam made air quotes with her hands— "to have to drive you everywhere because you fried your engine, then you need to keep on top of this." She wished she had a "distraction," especially during the holiday season.

"I will. Thanks for staying late."

The bells Sam had hung on the front door of the repair shop jingled, followed by the motion-detecting Santa playing his lively tune.

All Is Bright

"Go get 'em, worker boy." Sam wiped her hands on her shop rag and turned to wheel her cart over to her bright pink toolbox. She started putting the tools in the drawers when Axel appeared right next to her. She jumped and almost swore. "Dude, I should put some bells on you, too."

He laughed. "Sorry, boss. Didn't mean to scare you."

Yeah, right. He definitely didn't look sorry. "Did you take care of whoever was there?"

"He's still here. He says he wants to talk to you." Axel stood there. "He looks kind of familiar."

The man in the waiting room turned as she walked in. She tugged on her beanie, wishing she had at least looked in the mirror to check for grease smears on her face. Too late. Sam cleared her throat. "Excuse me, were you looking for me?"

His perfectly groomed eyebrows drew together as he looked at her and then he glanced away. "Um, no, I'm looking for Sam Gentry, the owner."

Of course he looked familiar to Axel. Pax Maughan had said that his brother would be coming into town. For some reason, she thought he wouldn't be here until after the first of the year. The man stood, waiting for her response.

She felt her face color as she pointed to the name patch on her uniform shirt. "Yeah, that's me. Samantha Gentry."

"Oh, sorry, I didn't know you were a . . . I mean, Patrick told me your repair shop took care of all our vehicles and I wanted to come check you—I mean check your business—out."

"Yes, we've had a good history with Bigger Valley." It didn't hurt that her shop, Gentry Auto, was right across the street from Bigger Valley Adventures.

"Good. Well, I'm Patrick's brother, Justin." He put out his hand like he wanted to shake hers but then quickly pulled it back and put his hands in his coat pockets.

Apparently, her hands were too dirty for him. Fine. "I didn't think you'd be here until after Christmas."

"I was able to get here a little sooner than expected." Justin

All Is Bright

looked around the shop again. "So, you're the owner?"

Why was a woman owning an auto repair shop so hard to believe? "I'm the owner. And the lead mechanic."

Justin looked skeptical. "Oh, okay. Well, thanks for your time." He turned and left the way he had come, the motion sensitive Santa not sounding so jolly.

All Is Bright
Chapter Two

It took finishing up Cam's car, changing out of her uniform, and being out in the cold evening air for Sam to cool down after talking to Justin Maughan. She was meeting Pax and his wife Merilee for dinner just down the street from both of their businesses. Even though the brothers looked a lot alike, they seemed totally different. Pax didn't have a problem working with a woman, why did his brother?

She walked through the door of the café, the warmth and Christmas music mellowing her out more. Merilee waved her over, her eight-month pregnant belly barely fitting in the booth. Sam's steps stuttered as she noticed that Mer and Pax weren't the only ones sitting there. Of course Justin would be there. She was tempted to turn around and walk out, but her stomach wouldn't let her. She was hungry.

"Thanks for waiting. I hope I didn't keep you long." She stood next to the booth.

Justin looked up at her, evidently as surprised as she had been to see him. She looked pointedly at his coat laying next to him.

His brown eyes widened and then he hurriedly put his coat between him and the wall. Sam slid in, perching on the edge of her seat.

She sat stiffly. Having known Pax for several years now, Sam was used to the long hair that was usually pulled back in a braid or a ponytail. His hair was lighter than Justin's, probably because he was out in the sun more. Justin had a very conservative short hairstyle. Everything about him screamed big city.

Pax had told her a little about their story. He had been nine and Justin twelve when their parents divorced. Justin had stayed with their dad in New York and Pax had followed their mom to Montana. It had been years since the brothers had seen each other.

Sam was focusing more on her guacamole burger than on

All Is Bright

the two men catching up. She was startled to find that everyone at the table was looking at her.

She quickly wiped her mouth with her napkin. "I'm sorry. What did I miss?"

Pax laughed. "I was just saying that I have a huge favor to ask you."

Sam smiled. "Favor? How huge?"

"Well, I know that tomorrow is your day off. Both Mer and I have to work, and Justin got here a little sooner than we expected. He really needs to get outfitted for our winter and I was wondering if you'd be able to take him around to get what he needs."

Ugh. Why did he have to ask her with Justin sitting right there? She really didn't want to spend time with an uptight guy from New York who probably wouldn't even last the winter here.

"Patrick, I can just find my way around. This town isn't so big that I'll get lost."

So, he didn't want to be with her either? Fine.

Merilee spoke up. "Don't be silly, Justin. Sam knows her way around town and knows what you'll need to stay warm and dry. You might end up taking people out on tours and you don't want to get stranded and freeze to death because you're not outfitted well enough."

Pax looked over at Sam, a pleading look in his eyes. "Please?"

Sam sighed. Hopefully, not a loud, offending sigh. "Okay, fine. I have nothing else planned for tomorrow."

All Is Bright
Chapter Three

Sam was running late. She knew she was in trouble when she pulled in front of Pax's house to find Justin pacing up and down the driveway. He came around the front to get into her Jeep and she noticed his eyes drawn to the Rudolph nose and antlers she always put on it for Christmas.

Sam turned down the Christmas music as he settled into his seat. "I'm so sorry. One of my neighbors couldn't get their car started, so I helped."

His mouth, which had been a hard line, relaxed slightly. "Well, that was nice."

"Yeah, occupational hazard." As she backed out of the driveway, she glanced over at Justin. "So, are you ready for this?"

This time he smiled. "Ready or not." He leaned a little closer to Sam. "I'm not a big fan of shopping," he whispered, like he was telling her a big secret.

Oh boy. This man was dangerous. "Yeah, but those stylish shoes and cashmere sweaters aren't too practical here in West Yellowstone."

He nodded. "You're right. Even though I'm used to a lot of snow, I'm not usually out in it for very long." He looked around him. "This is a nice Jeep."

"Thanks. It gets me where I need to go, and we have a good time doing it. What do you drive?" Probably some impractical luxury car.

"I don't drive. Remember? New York? City of expensive parking and public transportation?"

Oh yeah. "Wow. When I was about nine or ten my dad would have me pull cars in and out of the shop. I've basically been driving since then."

"Are you serious? You were working and driving that young?" He looked like he was ready to call CPS or something.

"Woah, slow down there. It wasn't really working. I'd come over after school and sometimes on Saturdays. All I'd do was

All Is Bright

drive the cars a few feet, put tools away, and help clean up. Besides, you can't call it work if you're not getting paid." She hesitated. "I guess I can't say I didn't get paid. I did make a whopping dollar an hour."

"A dollar an hour? That is some serious cash." He smiled over at her and she smiled back.

"If you don't mind me asking, if you and Pax lost contact, how did you end up here?"

He looked out his window. "Well, to tell the truth, watching my dad work himself to death two years ago, I realized that that was the path I was on." He turned to her. "I don't want the same thing. I want to live out my years, not just work them." He sighed. "Our parents divorce wasn't a good one, and Dad never talked about Mom and Patrick. It's taken me this long to work up the courage to contact my brother. I left everything behind in New York, and now Patrick wants me to stay with him until I figure out what I'm doing." He chuckled. "I guess I should start calling him Pax."

All Is Bright
Chapter Four

Shopping didn't take very long and went a lot smoother than Sam expected. She was actually surprised at how much she enjoyed spending time with Justin. After getting all the shopping bags in the Jeep, she turned to him. "Well, I don't know about you, but spending all your money sure took everything out of me. I'm starving."

"So, what do they have to eat here?"

"Probably nothing as fancy as you get in a big city, but there's a good variety. What do you feel like eating?" She hoped it was something close by and quick.

"That place we ate at last night wasn't bad. Is there something like that on our way?"

Sam thought for a second and flipped a u-turn. A strangled noise came from the passenger seat, and she looked over to see Justin clutching the handle above his door. "Hey, I checked to make sure no one was coming."

"Sorry. You'd think after riding in New York traffic that I wouldn't be startled by anything."

They made their way into the small diner and were seated at a booth again. Facing each other. Sam couldn't get over how much the two brothers looked like each other. If someone put Pax's long hair and scruff on Justin and made his brown eyes hazel, they'd be identical. It didn't help that she had had a long-term going nowhere crush on Pax.

"Sam." Justin looked frustrated, like he had just got done repeating her name. Oops.

"I'm sorry. What?" She gave him her full attention. Did he just ask if she had dated his brother?

"I asked if you knew what you were going to order."

Oh, phew. She didn't have to tell him that she had never dated Pax, or that she didn't date because just about everyone her age was already married, or that she wouldn't date tourists. "Sorry, no." Sam pretended to search the menu a little more, even though she already knew what she was going to get. "So,

All Is Bright

Pax is teaching you how to drive?"

"Yes. He doesn't want to be stuck driving me all over." Justin didn't look too excited. "I'm glad there's not very much snow on the ground."

"Yeah, you're lucky. We've usually had at least one big storm by now. It's almost like Mother Nature is saving up for a great big punch."

Justin knocked on the table. "Please don't wish that on us. Let me get my snow legs under me and hope we don't get anything big until next winter."

"You do know that your business depends on a lot of snow and tourists at this time of year." And her business depended on his business.

"I know, but if we could keep a consistent amount on the ground, that would be great."

That was so not going to happen.

All Is Bright
Chapter Five

Sam finished the test drive on the car she had been working on and pulled up to her shop. There was Justin sitting on a snowmobile right outside. She hadn't talked to him since their shopping trip over a week ago. She rolled up behind him and honked.

Justin jumped and almost fell off the machine.

Laughing, Sam got out of the car. "Hey stranger, what brings you over to my neck of the woods?" She was glad she looked more put together than when they first met. Her uniform shirt was tucked in, and instead of a beanie, she had a Christmas print bandana on her head, Rosie the Riveter style.

"Hey." He got off the snowmobile and took a couple of steps toward her. "We just had a group come back and they said this machine was having problems."

It shouldn't have bugged her that he was only here on business, but it did. "Let me finish up this car and then I'll get to it." She looked at the non-existent watch on her wrist. "Give me about a half hour."

He smiled "Thanks. It was good seeing you again, Sam." He turned and walked away, leaving her wishing he hadn't.

All Is Bright
Chapter Six

Samantha Joy Gentry needed her head examined, pure and simple. Since the time that Justin had brought that snowmobile over, they had seen each other almost every day or evening after work. He was so much more relaxed than when they first met and was becoming too much a regular part of her life. It scared her. She knew she was on the road to getting her heart broken if he ever decided to head back to the big city.

The other night when they had been hanging out at Pax and Merilee's, Justin had indicated that he had only been on the groomed snowmobile trails through the park. Because of her big mouth, she and Justin were now heading out to her property to spend the day snowmobiling.

"Have I told you how much I really like your Jeep?" Justin was drumming his fingers on the dash along with the song about the drummer boy.

"Yes, only every time you get in. Have you thought about getting your own vehicle? I could help you look." This would give her a little indication what his future plans were.

"Thanks, but while I'm living and working with Pax, I don't need a vehicle. Plus, Pax said that any time I need to, I could borrow one of theirs."

If he had his own house or at least his own car, then that would be more of a sign that he was staying put. Sam needed to distance herself from him, but with Christmas being a few days away and just really enjoying being with him, she couldn't. She was tempted to just turn around and make up an excuse, but they were already to her property. She turned off the highway and put her Jeep in 4-wheel drive. She hadn't been here since the last snow. Driving through the trees, they got to the house that she grew up in. She pulled in front of the garage and turned off the Jeep.

"Is this where you live when you're not staying in town?" Justin had been to the room she rented during the week.

"No, this is the house where I lived with my dad. It's empty.

All Is Bright

My house is back there a little bit." She swung her hand to her left, knowing he wouldn't be able to see it from there.

She got out of the Jeep and opened the garage. Inside was a snowmobile, a four-wheeler, and a side by side.

"Nice toys." Justin had grabbed his helmet and joined her in the garage.

She smiled over at him. "Thanks. There's more at my place."

He quirked an eyebrow at her. "Okay, so which one do I get to drive?"

"We're both riding the snowmobile up to my house and then we'll get the other one." She put her gloves on, got on the machine, and drove it out of the garage. Justin pulled the garage door down as she put her helmet and goggles on.

"So, how big is your property?" He put his helmet on and slid on behind her.

"It's about fifty acres. It used to be a lot more, but I sold off part of it." She started up the snowmobile. "Hang on."

She took off through the trees, more familiar with this land than she was with what was under the hood of a car, and she knew a lot about cars. Justin was holding onto the handles under the seat rather than wrapping his arms around her. There was a flash of disappointment, but the feel of his warm body so close to her was already a little too much. She drifted to the left and they were soon in an open area. It was time to fly. She watched the speedometer as it rose. She laughed as Justin whooped and hollered. He probably had never gone this fast on one of their tours. She sailed over the untouched powder for a little way more, and right before they reached the tree line, she slowed and then banked hard to the left.

The warmth of Justin's body was no longer present behind her. She turned around and drove slowly toward where she lost him. Suddenly, a form rose out of the snow and started shaking itself off. She couldn't go any further, she was laughing so hard.

"Did you do that on purpose?" Justin's voice rang through

All Is Bright

the open area.

She laughed even harder. Next thing she knew, she was pulled off the snowmobile and thrown into the snow. She came up sputtering only to be pelted with snowballs. Sam held up her hands. "Truce!"

She lay back in the snow and started a snow angel. Justin followed suit a few feet away.

"You know, when you launched me, my life flashed before my eyes. Then right before I landed, I realized I wasn't going to get hurt, and it was the most exhilarating thing I've ever done."

She looked over at him and felt as if she was flying through the air. She didn't know if she would have as soft a landing as he did. Getting up, she walked over and extended her hand. "Truce, remember?"

He grabbed her hand and acted like he was going to pull her down, but then stood up. He didn't let go until they got back to the snowmobile. He climbed onto the front, patted the seat behind him. "Just tell me where to go. You are no longer trustworthy."

She climbed on and wrapped her arms around him tightly. "Okay, but just to warn you, if you try what I did, we'll both fly off."

"Oh, don't worry, I'd probably hurt us both if I tried that. Just direct me where I need to go, speed demon."

She did, trying to ignore how good it felt to be so close to him. Luckily, it didn't take long until they were pulling up to her house.

All Is Bright
Chapter Seven

Sam loved the house she had helped build. The only time she lived in town was during the worst parts of winter. The snowstorms were too unpredictable, and she couldn't afford to be stranded out here for very long.

Justin whistled when she opened her garage, revealing another snowmobile and four-wheeler, along with a couple of kayaks. "Wow, you really do have more toys."

"Yeah, but they're essential toys. I need them to go back and forth between houses."

"The kayaks, too?" He winked at her.

She stuck her tongue out at him.

Justin laughed. "So, no one lives in the other house?"

"Pax and Merilee sometimes stay in it if we're out here playing and they don't want to drive back into town. This is pretty much our playground year-round."

He looked around. "I can see why."

Sam backed the other snowmobile out of the garage and left the door open. "Are you ready for some more riding? I promise I'll go slower for you." She grinned.

"Yes, where are we going?"

"I want to show you something." She took off, going slow enough that Justin was able to keep up with her. As they came to a rise, she slowed even more to crest it. They stopped at a break in the trees.

Justin took off his helmet as he took in the view in front of them and slowly got off his seat, a look of wonder on his face. They could see down into Yellowstone, the colors of the trees and hot pots a stark contrast to the bright white snow. Several animals also dotted the landscape.

Sam joined him, and he took her hand in his again. She could feel the warmth of his hand, even through their gloves, and she leaned into his side. The wind started to rustle the leaves, but other than that it was silent.

"This is amazing." Justin looked down at her. "Thank you

for bringing me up here."

She met his gaze. "You're welcome." Her voice was quiet. The energy around them shifted, almost as if another type of storm was coming.

He pulled her closer with his right hand, and with his left hand on her shoulder, angled her close to him. He slowly placed his lips on hers, blending his breath with hers. He added more pressure and she responded, wrapping her arms around his waist. He deepened the kiss and ran his fingers through her short hair.

Sam moaned against his mouth and his hands traveled down her back to pull her closer, his kisses pressed to her cheek, her earlobes, her neck. He started making his way back to her mouth. She was drowning and had to stop this.

He looked startled when she pulled away, heavily breathing.

She was shaking and couldn't look at him. "Justin, I can't do this."

He took a step toward her, and she backed up. "What do you mean? I thought you were doing a pretty good job." His voice was husky. Ugh. Way too sexy.

"No, I just can't. I'm sorry."

All Is Bright
Chapter Eight

What had she done? She was falling for someone who still didn't know what he was going to do. There were no indications he was staying permanently, and her heart was shattering. The wind had really picked up by the time they got to her house, so they pulled her snowmobile into the garage, and she shut the door.

Justin slid to the back of the seat and she climbed in front of him. He put his arms around her, and she had to fight off tears. She couldn't cry now; she'd have time to be emotional once she got to her room in town. Visibility wasn't very good once they got in her Jeep, but there was no way she'd be stuck here with Justin if a big storm was coming in.

They were both silent as they slowly made their way into town. Even though her eyes were glued to the road, she could feel him looking over at her. It was a relief when they pulled in front of Pax's.

Justin sat for a minute. "Sam, will you look at me?"

She finally did. "I'm sorry, Justin, but I've got to get home."

He breathed a sigh. "Will I see you Christmas Eve?"

Ugh. Christmas Eve was in three days. She spent every Christmas Eve with the Maughans. Sometimes, she'd come over on Christmas Day or they'd come to her place.

"Yes, I'll be there. I don't know how long I'll stay, though. It looks like our big storm is coming in." That was all she could give him.

He nodded and hurriedly got out of the Jeep, some snow blowing in before he got the door shut. She didn't make it to her rented room before the tears started falling.

All Is Bright
Chapter Nine

The big storm hit on Christmas Eve, just as the weathermen had predicted. Sam hadn't heard anything from Justin. She had only known him for a month, but she couldn't stop thinking about him. She had missed him, and it was harder than anything when she was working to not look across the street to see if she could catch any glimpse of him.

It was snowing heavily as she pulled up to Pax and Merilee's. Good, she'd have an excuse to leave early. She hurried through the front door, hanging her coat on a hook in the hall.

She took a deep breath and put a smile on her face as she rounded the corner into the kitchen. "Merry Christmas!"

"Merry Christmas." Merilee was finishing up dinner in the kitchen.

Sam gave her very pregnant friend a hug. "I can't believe you wouldn't let me help with anything."

"Well, I am nesting. Plus, we all know you're great with cars but in the kitchen, not so much." Mer laughed. "I just wanted to have this last hoorah before this little one comes along." She rubbed her belly.

"Well, can I do something?"

"Table is set, and dinner is ready. Do you want to start taking food in?" Merilee looked tired. The camera shop she owned must have been busy.

After putting the dishes on the table, Sam turned and waved at Pax and Justin who were in the family room. She went back into the kitchen.

"Is the snow still coming down?"

"Yes, it was picking up when I got here. I don't know how long I'll stay."

Merilee seemed disappointed, but Sam knew she understood the weather. She didn't know if Mer would understand that Sam couldn't spend much time with her brother-in-law.

Setting more food on the table, Sam overheard the two brothers talking quietly. Justin was saying something about

All Is Bright

hearing from New York and they wanted him back. The breath squeezed out of her chest. She couldn't stay any longer and pretend she was okay. She hurried into the entryway, grabbed her bag of gifts, and took them into the kitchen to Merilee.

"I'm sorry, Mer. I've got a headache and I really don't want to deal with this storm. I'm just going to head home. I'm sorry." She turned and went to the front door, slipping her boots on and barely getting her coat around her before she went out into the blizzard.

Since she had a few days off for Christmas, she had planned on going home. There was no way now that she was going to make it, and she had enough food in her room to last her for a couple of days, so she headed to her rented room.

She had just cried herself to sleep when her phone started ringing, waking her up. She groggily looked at the display. It was Merilee.

She cleared her throat. "Hello?"

"Sam, where are you? Are you at your house or here in town?" Her voice was frantic.

"I'm here in town. Why?"

"Is Justin with you?"

"No, why—?"

"Sam, Justin left an hour ago, saying he was going to your place. I thought he was going to your room, and I didn't want to bug you, but now I'm scared. We've tried calling him, but he's not answering." Merilee sounded like she was in tears. "Pax is planning on going out to find him."

Sam flew out of bed and was already getting dressed. "Mer, don't let Pax go. He needs to stay with you. I'll go find him. Besides, I'm more familiar with that stretch of road than Pax is."

"Okay, come by here first. I'm going to have Pax grab some of Justin's clothes, and I'll throw something together for you." Merilee's voice broke. "Please find him."

"I will. I'll be right over." She could hear Merilee's shouted instructions to Pax as she hung up. She quickly went through

All Is Bright

a mental checklist of the emergency supplies she kept in her Jeep and then braced herself for the short walk in the blizzard.

The trip to Pax's took a few minutes longer than usual, and as she pulled into his driveway, Pax came running out with a large duffel bag under one arm and some blankets under the other. He opened her passenger door and she helped him situate his load into her backseat.

"I just got my brother back. Please find him." Pax shut the door, and she didn't even wait until he had gotten into his house before she was on her way.

Sam inched along the highway carefully, thankful for the tall poles placed so that drivers could know where the road was in just this situation.

Her hands were hurting with how hard she gripped her steering wheel and she lost track of how far she had gone. Suddenly there was a snowbank that looked like it had a dim light coming from it. It had to be Pax's truck with Justin in it. She had just passed a pole, and the truck seemed to be off the road a few feet. She pulled up beside the mound and got out of her Jeep, leaving it running. She hurried over to where the driver's door should be and started scraping snow off the window. The window was fogged but she could make out someone inside. She knocked on the window and the person turned slowly.

It was Justin.

All Is Bright
Chapter Ten

She pulled on the handle. It was locked. "Justin, open the door." She knocked on the window.

He looked disoriented, and she noticed a dark stain on his face. Her heart stopped. It was blood.

She pounded this time. "Justin, let me in."

It seemed to finally register that she was there. He slowly reached over and opened the door, half falling out. The truck was not running, and Justin was cold. Why hadn't he kept the engine going? With him leaning on her, they made the few feet to her Jeep and she opened the passenger door, helping him in and strapping his seatbelt on. She was about to shut his door when he grabbed her arm.

"I need the bag."

"Justin, we need to go. You're bleeding."

"Get the bag." He leaned his head back.

"Okay, I'll get it. Don't fall asleep." She shut his door and looked in Pax's truck. On the floor on the passenger side was a shopping bag. Sam grabbed it and put it in the back of the Jeep. She placed two telescoping poles by the truck so it wouldn't get hit by snowplows. She turned off the headlights, locked the door, and jumped in her Jeep. Justin's eyes were still closed, but the bleeding from his forehead appeared to be slowing down.

She wrapped him in a couple of blankets. "Justin." She nudged him. "You can't go to sleep."

He opened his eyes slightly. "Did you get the bag?"

"Yes, please stay awake." She couldn't watch him and watch the road, and she didn't want to be stuck out here in the blizzard. She had to keep talking to him.

"What happened to you, Justin? How did you hurt your head?"

His hand went up slowly and back down again. "I think I hit a deer."

It was possible. The impact had probably damaged the radiator, which was probably why the truck wasn't running.

All Is Bright

Thankfully, he wasn't going fast because of the snow, or there could have been more damage. Justin shivered. Sam turned the heater up more.

"Why did you leave?" He turned toward her.

"We're not talking about that right now. I just want to get you safe. Where is your phone?" She hadn't seen it.

"I don't know." He opened his eyes and looked out the windshield. He groaned and shut his eyes again. "Where are we going?"

"The house I grew up in." The snow had let up slightly and she saw some familiar trees. "We're almost there."

Sam almost sobbed with joy when they got to the house. She nudged Justin again. He had been quiet for a few minutes. "Justin, we're here. I need you to wake up. I can't carry you."

He was shaking, even though the Jeep was warm. "Okay," he mumbled. "Get the bag."

She had almost forgotten the blasted bag. "Alright. I have to get out to open the garage. Please stay awake." He grunted.

As fast as she could, Sam pulled into the garage and helped Justin into the house and onto the couch. "I'm going to leave you here for a minute while I start a fire and get some stuff out of my Jeep. Stay awake."

He gave her a thumbs up.

Sam got a fire going in the fireplace and was grateful she had made sure the house was ready for winter. She called Pax and let them know they were staying put. By the time she had gotten everything out of the Jeep, the house was already starting to warm up. She kept up conversation with Justin, even though he was getting irate. He just wanted to sleep. After putting another couple of blankets on him, she put away the food that Merilee had packed. There was enough to keep an army fed for a month.

Justin was still shivering as she sat next to him and gently cleaned the blood off his face. The wound wasn't very big and had stopped bleeding, so Sam bandaged it up the best she could. She called Pax and let him know they were safe and hunkering down.

Sam pulled a mattress off one of the beds and dragged it in front of the fire. Before helping him out of his coat and boots, she checked Justin's pupils. They looked normal. Some of the tightness loosened in her chest. She settled him on their makeshift bed and then ran back into her old bedroom to change into a pair of sweatpants and a t-shirt. She shivered all the way back into the family room and climbed under the blankets with Justin, keeping him between her and the fire. She wrapped her arms around him and wished her body heat onto him. It took a little while for his shivering to settle down. She was finally able to relax when he started softly snoring. It was a sound she could get used to, and she tried not to let her crying wake him as she realized the time they had alone in her house would be the only time she would hear it.

All Is Bright
Chapter Eleven

Sam must have finally drifted off to sleep because when she woke up, she could tell the fire was almost out, and there was a delicious smell coming from the kitchen. The heat from Justin's body was no longer there either.

She got up and made her way into the kitchen, wiping the sleep from her eyes. Justin was dressed and standing at the stove with his back to her. "Good morning."

Justin turned. "Merry Christmas." He looked a lot better this morning.

"Merry Christmas. It sure smells good in here." She ran her fingers through her hair, just imagining how matted to her head it probably was.

"If you want to shower, there's time before food is ready."

He didn't have to ask twice. Twenty minutes later Sam was back in the kitchen, wet spiky hair and all.

Justin motioned to the table that was already set. "Let's eat."

Sam sat down, amazed at the freshly baked blueberry muffins, hash browns, and bacon.

When she was totally stuffed, they went in and did the dishes together. Even though she was glad that he was helping, it was hard being in such close proximity to Justin. He was going back to New York and she would be left behind. Again.

There was no visibility out the kitchen window. This was the big storm, and they would be stuck here at least until tomorrow. "Well, great Christmas this has turned out to be," Sam mumbled.

"What's so bad about it? We're somewhere warm, the company is good," —Justin pointed to himself and winked— "and I found some games in one of the kitchen cabinets. We're safe and okay."

She wasn't okay. But instead of locking herself in her old bedroom and crying, she needed to figure out something to do.

"Oh, it's Christmas!"

All Is Bright

Justin laughed. "I thought we already established that."

"Yeah, we did, but Christmas means presents. I'll be right back." Sam slipped on her boots and went out to her Jeep, grabbing the large flat gift from behind the seats. As she got back into the family room, she noticed Justin's bag that he had been so insistent she bring in.

She motioned for him to sit on the couch. "Without a tree or decorations, it doesn't seem much like Christmas, but I got you something." She handed him the present.

He ripped the butcher paper off and turned the canvas over so he could see it. His eyes widened. "When did you take this?" His voice was quiet.

"I came back that next day. There was a break in the wind, so it was perfect. You were affected by that view, and I wanted you to have something to remember it by when you go back to New York."

He sat and stared for a moment at the canvas. Sam had taken a picture from her favorite place on her property and had Merilee print it up at her camera shop.

Justin got off the couch and in two steps was taking Sam in his arms. "Thank you."

She stiffened. This wasn't supposed to happen. Time stood still as he bent and kissed her lightly. Once. Twice. Something broke inside her, and she wrapped her arms around his neck and gave him every bit of her heart with her kiss. She didn't care if he was going to rip it out of her chest when he went back to New York. She didn't realize that she was crying until Justin pulled back, out of breath. He wiped her tears gently with his thumbs.

"Sam, what's wrong?"

She closed her eyes, not wanting to look into his. "I don't want you to go."

"Go where? I'm not going anywhere in this weather." He hugged her against him.

"No, I don't want you to go to New York." She sobbed into his chest.

All Is Bright

"New York?" He pushed her away slightly. "That's the second time you've mentioned New York. Sam, look at me."

She did.

"Who said I was going to New York?"

She closed her eyes again. "I heard you telling Pax that they wanted you back at your old job." She burrowed into him.

He sighed. "And did you stick around long enough to hear me tell Pax that I turned them down? No, you ran out into the storm, worrying us all and leaving me on Christmas Eve when all I wanted was to tell you I was staying. Here. Hopefully to be with you."

Her tears stopped, and she was the one to pull away this time. "You turned them down? You're staying? For good?"

His lips on hers answered her. It was a few minutes before they came up for air.

Justin guided Sam to the couch and had her sit down. Bending over, he picked up the all-important bag, pulling two presents out of it.

He handed her the smaller gift and sat beside her. She hurried and opened it. It was one of the nicer cameras from Merilee's shop that she had wanted for a while. "How did you know?"

Justin smiled. "Merilee showed me some pictures you took that she has hanging in her store. She also said you've been eyeing this camera, but you probably would never buy it for yourself."

Merilee wasn't wrong.

He then handed her the other present, which was the size of a shoebox. Sam unwrapped it only to find . . . a shoebox. Taking the lid off, she was confused to find Justin's expensive leather loafers. What?

"Do you know what this is?" Justin put his arms around her and pulled her into his side.

She could feel her pulse thrumming through her chest. "Your shoes?" she asked, breathlessly.

He chuckled. "Well, yes, but they're also a sign that I'm not

All Is Bright

going anywhere." He pointed to the large print she had given him. "Do you know why I loved that view so much and why I love this picture?" Sam shook her head. "Because this was where and when I knew that this was where I would be staying. I have finally found my home." He turned her toward him. "And I have found someone I'd like to have a future with."

Sam hoped that her lips on his was answer enough. Even as unconventional as it was, this was turning out to be her best Christmas ever.

About the Author

Lori Widdison was raised in Albuquerque, New Mexico where she developed her love of books and sunsets/sunrises. She has lived most of her adult life in Utah, close to the Wasatch Mountains, and her husband tolerates her above mentioned other loves. When she isn't crafting, writing, reading, or trying to stay connected to her adult children and young grandchildren, she is binging on Korean and Chinese dramas. Even though she mostly reads fantasy and mystery, the only thing that comes out of Lori's brain is romance.

Anonymous

by Anonymous

Every year at Christmas, my family did something special—and anonymous—for someone we knew. Sometimes we did the "12 Days of Christmas," where you leave a little something on the same doorstep every night for twelve nights with a silly little rhyme similar to the Christmas carol along with a small gift. To make sure we were anonymous and that no one could ever figure out the handwriting, we typed each night's message on a 3x5 card.

For my mom, the hard part was probably coming up with the rhyme to correspond with the small gift. For me, the hard part was being "the runner." In past years, our usual routine was to try to switch up the times of delivery so as not to be caught. My dad would sometimes leave the gift on his early morning runs so that I wouldn't have to deliver at the same time every night, in fact. But for some reason, that year it seemed like every night the task fell to me.

Often, the layout of the doorstep was the most impossible placement I could envision. The apartment building of the family we had chosen had an open central courtyard with the stairwell to the upstairs apartments—which is exactly where

All Is Bright

they lived, in an upstairs unit that looked directly over the stairwell and the street. My mom must have had to call upon her deepest reserves of patience with me that year. The street was curved and narrow with not a lot of turnaround room. I'm sure we must have had to drive by what seemed like a dozen times every night until I mustered the courage to make the delivery. I would get so nervous, my heart racing with the fear of being seen or caught at the door. When the time arrived, or my mom had decided enough was enough, I'd have to jump out of the car, race up the stairs, set down the gift, knock and then dash away and hopefully not stumble down the stairs on my escape.

After all this effort and stealth and I'm sure at least a few tears, what made this year different, that we felt like we wanted to share our identities with our recipients? I was shocked when even my parents agreed to disclose ourselves. This wasn't like them at all. They loved to serve without acknowledgement. But this year seemed different.

We had chosen a fun, young couple we knew from church. There was just something special about them and we knew they would be like all the other young couples in our congregation—they wouldn't stay. They were young and just starting out in life and I wouldn't know them for long, but I would always remember them and this Christmas. So as a family, we decided we would give them their final 12th Day gift after church on Christmas Eve Sunday.

We told them we wanted to see them after church was over, that we had something for them.

Our anticipation grew as we waited to speak to them, but we let others go first so that there would be fewer people around when we told them. But how would this work? What would we say?

As we quickly found out, we didn't have to say anything. All we did was pull the gift out from our bag and they saw the typed note on the 3x5 card and that was all they needed.

You could see it in their eyes.

All Is Bright

They knew.

I'm sure something must have been said, but it wasn't necessary. We cried and hugged and I think we all felt part of something special that 12th day of Christmas. All those hard nights of struggling to make the delivery without being caught no longer seemed to matter. I could tell that it had meant something special to them to be on the other side of that door, waiting in anticipation to receive each delivery.

Made in the USA
Monee, IL
29 November 2020